The Dark Queen's Curse

Fairy tales, Folk tales, Legends & Mythology, Volume 9

Patrick William Lee

Published by Starlit Tales Publishing, 2024.

THE DARK QUEEN'S CURSE

First edition. September 4, 2024.

Copyright © 2024 Patrick William Lee.

ISBN: 979-8227878540

Written by Patrick William Lee.

Table of Contents

To those who find light in the darkest of places,

Who face impossible choices with unwavering courage,

And who never stop believing in the magic of hope.

This is for you.

Chapter 1: The Rise of the Dark Queen

In a land once rich with verdant fields and serene rivers, there was peace. The kingdom of Eldore, nestled between two towering mountain ranges, had known prosperity for centuries. Its people lived in harmony, thriving under the benevolent rule of King Lorian and Queen Aeliana, who were as just and fair as they were beloved. But every peace has its shadow, and within the court of Eldore, a darkness had begun to fester. That darkness was Morgana, the queen's youngest sister—one whose fate was forever altered by a deep thirst for power and the forbidden magic that would eventually consume her.

Morgana had always been different. Even as a child, she possessed a quiet intensity that unnerved her peers. While her sisters played in the sun-dappled gardens or learned the art of diplomacy from their mother, Morgana sought solitude. She preferred the ancient libraries of Eldore, where she pored over forgotten tomes and esoteric scrolls. Her curiosity was insatiable, and the more she learned, the more she craved. But it wasn't simply knowledge that Morgana sought—it was power.

There was a darkness in Morgana, one that neither her sisters nor her parents could comprehend. It was as if the light of Eldore never quite reached her. Where Queen Aeliana radiated warmth and compassion, Morgana embodied cold ambition. Her once soft features became harder with each passing year, her eyes glinting with a strange, unfathomable intensity that unsettled those around her. And as Morgana matured, so too did her desire to break free from the limitations of mortal life. She longed for something more, something transcendent.

One fateful evening, Morgana stumbled upon a book long forgotten in the deepest corner of the royal library. Bound in weathered leather and marked with cryptic symbols, the tome seemed to pulse with an otherworldly energy.

Its title, inscribed in an ancient script, translated to *The Arcane Path: The Secrets of Forbidden Magic*. Morgana's heart raced as she opened the book, her fingers trembling with anticipation. She knew the dangers of dabbling in such magic, for the ancient laws of Eldore strictly forbade the study and practice of dark sorcery. But Morgana had never cared much for rules.

Within the pages of the ancient tome lay the key to unlocking the power she so desperately craved. The text spoke of rituals to summon forces beyond comprehension, forces capable of granting unimaginable strength to those willing to pay the price. Morgana read the passages with a mixture of fear and exhilaration, knowing that once she walked this path, there would be no turning back.

In the dead of night, when the moon hung high in the sky like a silver blade, Morgana began her dark descent. She ventured deep into the forest beyond the castle walls, where the air grew thick with magic and the trees whispered secrets of old. At the heart of the forest lay a circle of ancient stones, a place where the veil between worlds was thin. It was here that Morgana performed the ritual, chanting words from the forbidden tome as the wind howled around her.

The ground beneath her feet began to tremble, and the air crackled with energy. Morgana's eyes widened as a dark figure materialized before her, a being of shadow and malice. The figure's voice was like the rustling of dead leaves, cold and hollow, as it asked her the question that would seal her fate:

"What do you desire?"

MORGANA DID NOT HESITATE. "Power," she replied, her voice steady and unwavering. "I desire the power to rule, to bend the world to my will."

The figure regarded her for a moment, its eyes glowing with a sinister light. *"Power comes at a price,"* it said. *"Are you willing to pay it?"*

Morgana nodded. She had already made her decision. Whatever the cost, she would pay it.

The dark figure smiled, and with a wave of its hand, the pact was sealed. A searing pain shot through Morgana's chest as the ancient magic took hold of her, binding her soul to the forces of darkness. She screamed, collapsing to the ground as the power coursed through her veins, transforming her into something more than mortal. Her once fair skin darkened, her eyes turning an unnatural shade of black. When she rose, she was no longer Morgana. She had become something far more dangerous. She had become the Dark Queen.

THE TRANSFORMATION was swift, and soon, the kingdom of Eldore began to feel the effects of Morgana's rise. The first sign was the change in the weather. What had once been a land of gentle seasons and abundant harvests became plagued by violent storms and bitter winds. Crops withered in the fields, and rivers ran dry as a strange blight spread across the kingdom. The people grew restless, and whispers of Morgana's newfound power began to circulate.

But it wasn't just the land that suffered. Morgana's presence within the royal court became a source of fear and unease. King Lorian and Queen Aeliana were troubled by the transformation in their youngest sister, who now exuded an aura of menace wherever she went. Morgana no longer spoke in the soft, measured tones they had known; her voice was cold and commanding, her words sharp as daggers.

In the months following her dark ascension, Morgana began to make her move. She manipulated the court, sowing seeds of discord among the nobles and turning once-loyal allies against each other. Those who opposed her found themselves mysteriously afflicted by illness or plagued by nightmarish visions. It wasn't long before Morgana's influence extended beyond the castle walls. Villages on the outskirts of the kingdom reported strange occurrences—cattle dying without explanation, children disappearing in the night, and eerie figures seen lurking at the edges of the forest.

The Dark Queen's grip tightened with every passing day, but it was not enough for Morgana to rule from the shadows. She craved the throne itself, and she knew that in order to take it, she would have to eliminate the one obstacle standing in her way: her sister, Queen Aeliana.

It was a cold winter's night when Morgana made her final move. The castle was silent, save for the soft crackling of the fire in the great hall. Morgana stood before the throne, her black robes billowing around her like the wings of a raven. She gazed up at the ornate chair, her lips curling into a smile. Soon, it would be hers.

As if on cue, Queen Aeliana entered the hall, her face pale and drawn. She had felt the shift in the air, the growing darkness that emanated from her sister, and she had come to confront her one final time.

"Morgana," Aeliana began, her voice trembling with emotion, "what have you done?"

Morgana turned to face her sister, her eyes gleaming with malevolent power. "What needed to be done," she replied coldly. "I have embraced the power that was always meant to be mine. You and Lorian were too weak to see it, too blind to understand the true potential of magic."

Aeliana's heart ached as she looked at the woman who had once been her beloved sister, now twisted beyond recognition. "This is not power, Morgana," she said softly. "This is corruption. You have made a pact with forces that will destroy you."

Morgana laughed, the sound echoing through the empty hall. "Destroy me? No, dear sister. They have made me invincible. I have become the Dark Queen, and I will rule this kingdom as it was meant to be ruled—with strength, with fear, and with absolute power."

Aeliana shook her head, tears welling in her eyes. "You do not understand the cost of what you have done. The darkness will consume you, Morgana. It will devour everything that is good within you."

But Morgana was beyond reason. She raised her hand, and the air around her crackled with dark energy. "It is you who does not understand, Aeliana. You have ruled for too long, and your time has come to an end."

Aeliana had no chance to defend herself. With a flick of her wrist, Morgana unleashed a torrent of dark magic, striking her sister with a force that sent her crashing to the ground. Aeliana cried out in pain, her body convulsing as the magic tore through her.

But even in her final moments, Aeliana did not beg for her life. She looked up at Morgana, her gaze filled with sorrow and love. "I forgive you, Morgana," she whispered, her voice barely audible. "I only pray that one day, you will find the light again."

With that, Queen Aeliana's life slipped away, leaving Morgana standing alone in the great hall, the weight of her actions pressing down on her like a heavy shroud.

For a brief moment, Morgana hesitated. A flicker of doubt crossed her mind as she stared at her sister's lifeless body. Had she gone too far? Was there still a part of her that could be saved?

But the darkness within her was too strong. The power she had gained from the forbidden magic was intoxicating, and it had already begun to consume her soul. Morgana banished the doubt from her mind and turned her gaze once more to the throne.

With slow, deliberate steps, she ascended the dais and sat upon the throne that had once belonged to her sister. The cold stone beneath her felt like a victory, and yet, there was an emptiness in her heart that even her newfound power could not fill.

The Dark Queen had risen, and with her ascent, the kingdom of Eldore would never be the same.

In the days that followed, Morgana consolidated her power. She declared herself the rightful ruler of Eldore, claiming that Queen Aeliana had died of a sudden illness. The people of the kingdom, already frightened by the strange occurrences plaguing their land, accepted her rule out of fear. Those who dared to question her met with swift and brutal punishment.

Morgana's reign was marked by terror. The skies above Eldore grew darker with each passing day, and the land itself seemed to wither under her rule. The once-beautiful forests turned twisted and gnarled, the rivers ran black with sludge, and the creatures of the night grew bolder and more dangerous. It was as if the very soul of the kingdom was being drained away.

But even as Morgana's power grew, so too did the whispers of rebellion. In the shadows, a small group of loyalists began to gather, determined to find a way to end the Dark Queen's reign. Among them was a young woman named Elara, who would one day rise to challenge the Queen and fulfill the prophecy of the Cursed Child.

But for now, Morgana ruled unchallenged. The Dark Queen had claimed her throne, and with it, she had bound herself to the forces of darkness that would one day seek to claim her soul.

The price of power, Morgana would soon learn, was far greater than she could have ever imagined.

Chapter 2: The Kingdom in Peril

The kingdom of Eldore, once a shining beacon of peace and prosperity, was no longer the idyllic land it had been before Morgana's rise to power. From the day she ascended to the throne, a slow but inevitable decay began to spread, as though the very essence of life in the kingdom was being sapped by the dark magic that coursed through her veins. The whispers of rebellion that had begun in the days following Queen Aeliana's mysterious death soon gave way to a deeper, more pervasive silence—the silence of fear.

At first, the changes were subtle. The weather grew colder, even in the height of summer. The once-lush fields surrounding the capital began to show signs of withering. Farmers who had spent generations tending their land could no longer explain why their crops were failing. The soil itself, once rich and fertile, had turned dry and brittle. And it wasn't just the crops—animals, too, began to suffer. Cattle that had roamed freely in green pastures became sickly and weak, their eyes clouded with a strange, lifeless sheen. The herds that had once been the pride of Eldore's agricultural industry dwindled to a fraction of their former size.

But it was not only the farmers and herders who felt the effects of the Queen's dark magic. The towns and villages that dotted the landscape of Eldore began to suffer in more sinister ways. Famine struck the northern provinces first, where the colder climate had always made farming a more precarious endeavor. Normally, the people of these provinces could rely on trade with the more temperate southern regions to make up for any shortfall in their harvests. But now, with crops failing throughout the kingdom, there was little to trade. The roads, once bustling with merchants and travelers, grew empty as caravans carrying food and supplies ceased to arrive.

The famine spread like wildfire, consuming village after village. Families who had never known hunger before were forced to ration what little food they had. Bread became a rare commodity, and even the wealthiest of nobles found themselves tightening their belts. Desperation grew, and with it came the first whispers of something far darker than mere hunger. Stories began to circulate of strange creatures seen in the forests at night—creatures with glowing eyes and twisted, unnatural forms. At first, these stories were dismissed as the ravings of frightened peasants. But as more and more sightings were reported, it became clear that something truly sinister was at play.

In the village of Hollowbrook, nestled at the edge of the Darkwood Forest, the fear was palpable. Hollowbrook had always been a peaceful, if somewhat isolated, community. Its people were used to living in harmony with the forest that surrounded them, relying on its bounty for food and resources. But the forest had changed. No longer a place of quiet beauty, it had become a place of dread, where shadows seemed to move of their own accord and strange noises echoed through the trees.

Mara, a young woman of eighteen winters, had grown up in Hollowbrook. She had always loved the forest, finding comfort in its towering trees and the gentle rustle of its leaves. But now, she could hardly bear to look at it. The once-familiar woods had taken on a sinister aspect, and the creatures that lurked within were no longer the harmless deer and rabbits she had known as a child. The villagers spoke of something else—something darker.

It had started with the livestock. Goats, chickens, and even the village's prized oxen had begun to disappear. At first, the villagers thought it was wolves, though wolves had not been seen in these parts for generations. But when the animals were found—what was left of them, at least—their bodies had been torn apart in ways that no wolf could have managed. Some were missing limbs, others their heads, and all had the same vacant, glassy-eyed stare, as though something had drained the life from them long before they died.

The villagers had set traps, of course. Hunters from the surrounding areas had been called in to track the creatures responsible. But no matter what they did, the attacks continued. Worse still, the hunters who ventured too far into the forest often did not return. And those who did were never the same. They spoke of seeing things—figures in the trees, shadows that moved with a will of their own. One hunter, a man named Jareth, had returned after three days missing, his face pale and gaunt. He refused to speak of what he had seen, but in the weeks that followed, his condition worsened. He grew thinner, his eyes sunken and hollow, and he began to suffer from terrible nightmares. He would wake in the middle of the night, screaming about "the eyes" and "the voices." No one could calm him. One morning, they found him dead in his bed, his body cold and stiff, his face twisted in a rictus of terror.

Jareth was not the only one. As the weeks passed, more and more villagers began to fall ill with a strange, wasting sickness. The symptoms were always the same: a sudden onset of weakness, followed by fever and chills. But it was the dreams that frightened the villagers the most. Those afflicted with the sickness all spoke of the same thing—of eyes watching them from the darkness, of voices whispering in a language they could not understand.

Mara's mother, a kind-hearted woman who had always cared for the sick and elderly, had been one of the first to fall ill. At first, Mara thought it was just exhaustion—her mother had been working tirelessly to care for the others in the village. But as the days passed and her mother grew weaker, Mara realized that this was no ordinary illness. Her mother's skin had taken on a greyish pallor, her once-bright eyes now dull and lifeless. And the dreams—Mara could see the fear in her mother's eyes every time she woke, drenched in sweat, from yet another nightmare.

Mara tried everything. She gathered herbs from the forest, consulted the village healer, and even prayed to the old gods for mercy. But nothing worked. Her mother's condition only worsened, and soon she was bedridden, too weak to even speak. Mara sat by her bedside, holding her mother's hand and whispering words of comfort, though in her heart she knew that nothing could save her.

The day her mother died, Mara felt something break inside her. She had never known a world without her mother's love and guidance, and now she was utterly alone. Her father had died when she was a child, and her older brother had left the village years ago to seek his fortune in the capital. Mara had written to him, begging him to return, but no letters had come in reply. It was as though the world outside Hollowbrook had forgotten them, just as they were being consumed by the darkness that surrounded them.

Hollowbrook was not the only village to suffer under the Dark Queen's rule. Across the kingdom, similar tales were being told. In the coastal town of Windshear, once a thriving port known for its bustling market and vibrant trade, the sea had turned against the people. The fishermen who had long relied on the bounty of the ocean found their nets coming up empty, and those who ventured too far from shore never returned. Strange lights had been seen in the water at night—pale, flickering orbs that seemed to move with an intelligence of their own. Some whispered that the lights were the spirits of drowned sailors, others said they were the work of sea witches. But whatever the cause, the result was the same: hunger and despair.

In the highland village of Greyspire, nestled at the foot of the Ironfang Mountains, the mines had run dry. For generations, the people of Greyspire had made their living by extracting precious metals from the mountains—iron, copper, and silver. But now, the veins had dried up, and the miners spoke of strange occurrences deep within the tunnels. Some claimed to hear voices whispering in the darkness, others reported seeing figures flitting just beyond the reach of their lanterns. The foreman, a grizzled veteran of the mines, had gone missing one night, and when his body was found, it was as though something had drained the very life from him. His skin was pale and shriveled, his eyes wide open in a look of pure terror.

The people of Eldore were suffering, and yet no one dared to speak out against the Queen. Her power had grown too great, and her wrath was swift and merciless. Those who dared to question her rule—whether they were noble or commoner—were never seen again. Some were said to be taken to the dungeons beneath the castle, where they were subjected to horrors beyond imagining. Others simply disappeared, their names erased from history as though they had never existed.

The Queen's enforcers, known as the Blackguard, were feared throughout the kingdom. Clad in dark armor and wielding cruel weapons, they patrolled the streets of the capital and the villages, ensuring that no one dared to rise against Morgana. The Blackguard were not ordinary soldiers—rumor had it that they had been corrupted by the same dark magic that had transformed Morgana. Their eyes glowed with an unnatural light, and they moved with an eerie, inhuman grace. Some said they were no longer men at all, but shadows given form by the Queen's will.

It wasn't just the Blackguard that the people feared, however. The unnatural creatures that had begun to appear in the forests and mountains of Eldore were far more terrifying. Some were described as twisted versions of familiar animals—wolves with too many eyes, deer with antlers made of bone and flame. Others were unlike anything the people had ever seen, monstrous beings with scales, claws, and teeth that could tear through steel. These creatures roamed the wilderness at night, and anyone unlucky enough to cross their path rarely lived to tell the tale.

One such creature, known only as the Night Beast, had been terrorizing the village of Blackmoor, a small settlement on the outskirts of the kingdom. The Night Beast was said to be as tall as a man, with the head of a wolf and the body of a serpent. Its eyes glowed red in the darkness, and its breath smelled of sulfur and death. It had already killed several villagers, and the people of Blackmoor lived in constant fear of its next attack.

Desperate for help, the village's mayor had sent word to the capital, begging the Queen to send soldiers to slay the beast. But no reply had come. The Queen, it seemed, cared little for the suffering of her people. Blackmoor was on its own.

In the capital city of Eldoria, the seat of Morgana's power, the atmosphere was no less grim. Once a bustling metropolis filled with laughter and music, the city had become a shadow of its former self. The grand markets, once brimming with merchants from across the land, now stood empty. The streets, once lively with the chatter of townsfolk, were now eerily silent. The only sounds were the heavy footsteps of the Blackguard as they patrolled the city, their presence a constant reminder of the Queen's iron-fisted rule.

Even the nobility, who had once enjoyed the luxuries of court life, had grown fearful. Morgana's court was no longer a place of revelry and diplomacy—it had become a den of paranoia and treachery. Those who had once been the Queen's closest advisors found themselves under constant scrutiny, afraid to speak out of turn for fear of incurring Morgana's wrath. The Queen had become increasingly volatile, her temper flaring at the slightest provocation. Some whispered that the dark magic she had used to seize power was beginning to consume her, driving her mad.

The palace itself had undergone a transformation. Where once it had been a place of light and beauty, with grand halls adorned with tapestries and gardens filled with vibrant flowers, it had now become a fortress of shadows. The walls seemed to pulse with a dark energy, and the very air inside the palace was thick with an oppressive, suffocating presence. Those who entered the throne room spoke of feeling an overwhelming sense of dread, as though the darkness itself was watching them.

Morgana sat upon her throne, her eyes gleaming with a cold, malevolent light. She had achieved everything she had set out to do—she was the Dark Queen, ruler of all Eldore. And yet, there was a hollow emptiness inside her, a gnawing sense of dissatisfaction that she could not shake. The power she had sought for so long now felt like a burden, weighing heavily upon her soul.

But Morgana could not turn back now. She had made her pact with the ancient forces of darkness, and there was no escaping the consequences. The kingdom was hers, but at what cost? The land withered under her rule, the people lived in fear, and her own soul was slowly being consumed by the very magic she had once craved.

As Morgana stared out the window of her throne room, watching the storm clouds gather on the horizon, she felt a flicker of doubt—a fleeting moment of uncertainty. But it was quickly snuffed out by the darkness that had taken root in her heart. There could be no turning back.

The kingdom of Eldore was in peril, and the Dark Queen's reign had only just begun.

Chapter 3: The Prophecy of the Cursed Child

The whispers of prophecy had long been woven into the fabric of Eldore's history. Ancient seers and scholars, their words etched into dusty scrolls, had foreseen great heroes rising in times of darkness, when the fate of the kingdom hung by the thinnest thread. These stories had always lingered on the edges of belief, filling the minds of peasants and nobles alike with hope when despair threatened to swallow them. But none was more feared, more revered, than the prophecy of the Cursed Child.

It was said to have been written centuries ago by an ancient oracle, a woman whose eyes had been blinded by the light of divine knowledge. Her name was lost to time, but her visions had been recorded by scribes who worked tirelessly to preserve the fragments of her foretellings. Of all her prophecies, the one that stood out, the one that survived the erosion of history, was the tale of the child born under the blood moon. This child, it was said, would bring an end to a reign of terror, breaking the curse that bound a powerful ruler to darkness.

For generations, the prophecy was little more than a story passed down from one generation to the next, a tale told around hearths on cold nights when families sought comfort in the idea that even the darkest of times could be undone by a single, miraculous event. But for Morgana, now the Dark Queen of Eldore, the prophecy was not a tale to be dismissed. It was a threat—a mortal danger to the power she had worked so hard to claim.

The prophecy began long before Morgana's rise, but its meaning had never felt more pertinent than now, as her reign stretched like a shadow over the kingdom. According to the ancient text, the child would be born on the night of the blood moon, a rare and ominous celestial event that occurred only once every few centuries. The child, marked by destiny, would possess the strength and magic to challenge a ruler of unmatched power—a ruler consumed by darkness.

The prophecy described the child as neither purely light nor entirely dark, a being forged in the balance of both worlds. It was said that the child's heart would be pure, but their power would be drawn from the same ancient forces that had corrupted the Dark Queen. This child would wield magic as old as time itself, able to break the chains of darkness that bound the ruler and bring balance back to the world.

To Morgana, who had gained her power through forbidden magic, the prophecy was a sword poised to strike at her heart. It was more than a simple warning; it was a glimpse of her undoing. For she, too, had drawn upon ancient forces to claim her throne, and now those same forces whispered of her downfall.

In the early days of her reign, Morgana had dismissed the prophecy as superstition, a relic of a bygone age. But as her power grew and the kingdom withered under her rule, she began to see the threads of fate aligning in ways she could not control. The signs of the blood moon's return became evident to those who studied the stars. Astrologers and mages began to speak in hushed tones of the celestial event, and Morgana, despite her disdain for the common people's beliefs, could not ignore the gnawing sense of inevitability.

One cold evening, while storms raged outside her castle, Morgana summoned her most trusted advisors to the throne room. The air was thick with tension as the Queen paced before them, her black robes trailing behind her like the shadows of death. The throne room, once a place of grand splendor, now felt like a tomb, its walls lined with the twisted remnants of tapestries that had long since decayed under the weight of her dark magic.

"Tell me," she hissed, her voice a sharp blade cutting through the silence, "what do you know of the blood moon?"

The advisors exchanged nervous glances, each one unwilling to be the first to speak. They had learned long ago that to speak too boldly in Morgana's presence was to invite punishment, but they had also learned that to stay silent was just as dangerous.

Finally, an elderly man with deep-set eyes and a trembling voice stepped forward. He was the court's chief astrologer, a man who had once served under

Morgana's sister, Queen Aeliana. His hands shook as he unrolled a parchment filled with star charts and calculations.

"Your Majesty," he began, his voice barely above a whisper, "the blood moon is... nearing. According to the charts, it will appear in the sky within the next few months."

Morgana's eyes narrowed, her gaze locking onto the old man like a predator stalking its prey. "And the prophecy?" she demanded. "The one that speaks of a child born under that cursed moon?"

The astrologer swallowed hard. "It is said, Your Majesty, that the child born on the night of the blood moon will be destined to end the reign of the ruler who has bound themselves to darkness."

Morgana's lip curled in a snarl. "Do you believe this prophecy, old man?"

The astrologer hesitated, knowing that his answer could seal his fate. "It is... only a legend, my Queen," he stammered. "But there are those who believe that such prophecies hold power, and that the stars themselves cannot be ignored."

Morgana turned away from him, her mind racing. She had known of the prophecy for years, but now, as the blood moon drew near, she could feel its weight pressing down on her. The forces she had bound herself to whispered in her ear, warning her of the child who would rise against her, and Morgana knew that she could not simply dismiss this threat.

"The child," she murmured, more to herself than to her advisors. "Where will they be born?"

The astrologer hesitated again. "That, we do not know, Your Majesty. The prophecy does not specify a location. It speaks only of the blood moon and the child's power."

Morgana clenched her fists, her nails digging into her palms. She could feel the darkness within her stirring, urging her to act. The blood moon was an omen, a sign that her reign, her very life, was in danger. She could not afford to be complacent.

"Then I will have to ensure that no such child is born," Morgana said, her voice cold and calculating. "Send word to every village, every town. No child born on the night of the blood moon will be spared."

Her advisors recoiled in shock, their faces pale with fear. Even they, who had long since become accustomed to Morgana's cruelty, could not hide their horror at her words.

"Your Majesty," one of them stammered, "you cannot mean to—"

"I do," Morgana interrupted, her eyes blazing with fury. "The prophecy will not come to pass. If there is even a chance that this child exists, I will root them out and destroy them before they can grow strong enough to challenge me."

The room fell into an uneasy silence as Morgana's words settled over them like a suffocating fog. None dared to oppose her. The Dark Queen had spoken, and her will would be done.

The following weeks were filled with chaos as Morgana's orders spread throughout the kingdom. Her enforcers, the dreaded Blackguard, marched from village to village, searching for any child born under the blood moon. The people, already living in fear of the Queen's dark magic, now faced a new horror: the loss of their children.

In the village of Westhaven, nestled at the foot of the Cragspire Mountains, the blood moon loomed large in the sky on the night of its arrival. The villagers, having heard the tales of Morgana's cruel decree, cowered in their homes, praying that the Queen's soldiers would not come for them.

But in a small cottage on the outskirts of the village, a child was born.

Her name was Elara.

She came into the world under the shadow of the blood moon, her first cries mingling with the howling wind that swept across the mountains. Her mother, a woman named Serah, held her newborn daughter close, tears streaming down her face. She had known the risks—everyone in the village had—but there had been no stopping the birth. The blood moon had chosen its time, and Serah could only hope that they would go unnoticed.

But fate, it seemed, had other plans.

As dawn broke over the village, the sound of horses' hooves echoed through the streets. The Blackguard had arrived, their dark armor gleaming in the morning light. Serah's heart raced as she heard the pounding on her door, her mind filled with the Queen's decree.

"Open in the name of the Queen!" a voice barked from outside.

Serah glanced at her husband, Edrin, who stood by the window, his face pale with fear. They both knew what this meant. The Blackguard had come for their child.

"We can't let them take her," Serah whispered, her voice trembling. "We have to hide her."

Edrin nodded, though his face was filled with uncertainty. "Where can we hide her? They'll search the whole house."

Serah's mind raced. There was no time to run, no time to plan. The Blackguard were already at the door. In a moment of desperation, she wrapped her newborn daughter in a thick blanket and handed her to Edrin.

"Take her to the cellar," she said, her voice barely audible. "There's a hidden compartment behind the barrels. They might not find her there."

Edrin hesitated for only a moment before nodding. He took the child and disappeared into the cellar, his footsteps echoing down the wooden stairs.

Serah composed herself, taking a deep breath as she approached the door. Her heart pounded in her chest, but she forced herself to remain calm. When she opened the door, she was met by the cold, expressionless faces of the Blackguard. Their leader, a tall man with a scar running down the side of his face, stepped forward.

"Is there a child born in this house last night?" he demanded, his voice devoid of any warmth or empathy.

Serah shook her head, her hands trembling at her sides. "No, my lord," she lied, her voice barely above a whisper. "There is no child here."

The Blackguard captain narrowed his eyes, studying her face for any sign of deception. Serah did her best to meet his gaze without flinching, but she could feel the weight of his scrutiny.

"We will search the house," the captain said after a long pause.

Serah nodded, stepping aside to allow the soldiers in. They moved through the cottage with practiced efficiency, searching every room, every corner. Serah stood frozen in place, her heart racing as they made their way toward the cellar. She prayed that they would not find the hidden compartment, that her daughter would remain safe.

But as the Blackguard captain descended into the cellar, Serah felt a sinking dread in her chest. Time seemed to stretch out, every second an eternity as she waited for the inevitable.

Then, she heard it—the sound of a barrel being moved, the scrape of wood against stone.

The captain emerged from the cellar, holding Elara in his arms.

Serah's breath caught in her throat as she saw her daughter in the hands of the Blackguard. The captain's expression remained unreadable as he looked down at the child, his scarred face a mask of indifference.

"This child was born under the blood moon," he said, his voice cold. "By the Queen's decree, she must be taken."

Serah felt a surge of panic rise within her. She moved toward the captain, her hands outstretched in a desperate plea. "Please," she begged, her voice breaking. "She's just a baby. She's innocent. Don't take her."

The captain's gaze shifted to Serah, and for a brief moment, she thought she saw something flicker in his eyes—pity, perhaps, or doubt. But whatever it was, it quickly vanished.

"The Queen's will is absolute," he said, his voice devoid of emotion. "No child born under the blood moon may live."

Before Serah could say another word, the captain turned and strode toward the door, Elara cradled in his arms. The other soldiers followed, their heavy boots thudding against the wooden floor as they left the cottage.

Serah fell to her knees, tears streaming down her face. She had failed. They had taken her daughter.

As the door slammed shut behind the Blackguard, Serah let out a heart-wrenching sob, her grief overwhelming her. She had known this day might come, but nothing could have prepared her for the reality of it.

But even in her despair, a flicker of hope remained. Elara was not just any child. She was the child of prophecy, born under the blood moon. And though Serah had lost her now, deep in her heart, she knew that Elara's destiny was far from over.

The Blackguard captain rode through the village with Elara in his arms, his expression unreadable. As he passed the terrified villagers, none dared to meet his gaze. They all knew what his presence meant, and they all feared what would come next.

But as the captain rode out of the village and into the dark forest beyond, a strange thing happened. The air around him seemed to grow heavier, the shadows deeper. He felt a chill run down his spine, though he could not explain why.

Then, without warning, the trees seemed to shift, the path before him twisting and turning in ways that defied logic. The captain pulled his horse to a stop, his heart pounding in his chest.

A figure stepped out of the shadows.

At first, the captain thought it was one of the forest's many creatures, a beast drawn to the scent of the child. But as the figure moved closer, he realized that it was something far more sinister.

The figure was cloaked in darkness, its face obscured by a hood. Its eyes glowed faintly, like embers in the night, and its presence seemed to suck the very light from the air around it.

"You will not take her," the figure said, its voice low and dangerous.

The captain's hand instinctively went to his sword, but before he could draw it, the figure raised a hand. The air around them seemed to ripple, and the captain felt an invisible force seize him, lifting him off his horse and throwing him to the ground.

Elara, still cradled in his arms, was unharmed. The figure moved forward, its movements swift and fluid, and took the child from the captain's grasp.

"She is the Cursed Child," the figure murmured, its voice filled with an eerie reverence. "The one who will break the Queen's curse."

Before the captain could react, the figure disappeared into the shadows, leaving him lying on the forest floor, gasping for breath.

He had failed.

Far away, in the depths of her dark palace, Morgana felt a sudden shift in the air. It was as though a thread in the great tapestry of fate had been tugged, altering the course of events in a way she could not foresee.

Her eyes narrowed, and she rose from her throne, her heart filled with a cold, simmering rage.

The prophecy was in motion.

And she would stop at nothing to prevent it from being fulfilled.

Chapter 4: The Forbidden Forest

Elara stood at the edge of the Forbidden Forest, her dark hair swept by the wind as she gazed into the dense canopy of trees that stretched endlessly before her. The forest was a place of legends, filled with whispers of ancient magic and unseen dangers. Its towering oaks, twisted pines, and the undergrowth that seemed to stretch out like grasping hands had long cast a shadow over the village of Ashbourne, where she had lived her entire life. For as long as Elara could remember, the forest had been forbidden to all but the most foolhardy. Yet, in that moment, the pull of its dark mysteries was stronger than the warnings she had been raised with.

Elara's family lived in a small cottage on the outskirts of Ashbourne, a village so remote that even traveling merchants rarely passed through. Her parents had passed when she was young, leaving her to be raised by the village healer, Moria, a woman who had taken Elara in as her own. Moria was kind and wise, her hands steady with the healing arts, but she had always been wary of the Forbidden Forest, as had everyone else in the village.

"Stay away from the forest," Moria had told Elara countless times, her voice heavy with the weight of caution. "No good comes from venturing into those woods. Many who enter never return, and those who do are changed."

As a child, Elara had heeded the warnings without question. She had played near the outskirts of the forest but never dared to step beyond the boundary where the trees grew thick and the light of the sun seemed to dim unnaturally. But as she grew older, curiosity began to tug at her, a curiosity that only grew stronger with time. The forest, with its secrets and its dark allure, called to her in ways she could not fully explain.

She was eighteen now, tall and lithe, with the fierce independence of someone who had learned to rely on herself from a young age. Her sharp green eyes missed little, and lately, she had noticed things—strange things—in the forest. There were shadows that moved where no person or animal should have been, whispers carried on the wind that spoke in a language she couldn't understand. Birds would fall silent at odd moments, their songs interrupted by a sense of foreboding. And sometimes, at night, Elara would catch glimpses of glowing lights deep within the woods, like eyes watching from the darkness.

The villagers often spoke in hushed tones about the Forbidden Forest, sharing stories of those who had vanished within its depths. Some claimed that it was home to spirits, others that it was cursed by ancient magic. But one thing was certain: no one who entered the forest ever did so willingly, and no one who ventured too far into its heart came back unchanged.

Elara, however, had never been one to shy away from danger or mystery. She had always felt different from the other villagers, though she couldn't quite put her finger on why. It wasn't just her curiosity or her longing for something beyond the mundane life of the village—it was a deeper feeling, a sense that she was connected to something greater, something just out of reach.

That morning, Elara had set out to gather herbs for Moria, as she often did, but she had found herself drawn to the edge of the forest. The basket she carried now hung loosely from her arm, forgotten, as her thoughts drifted toward the forest's depths. The wind stirred the leaves, creating a soft rustling sound that reminded her of whispers.

She took a step forward, her heart quickening. The villagers would think her mad for even considering entering the Forbidden Forest, but she couldn't shake the feeling that something was calling to her from within. Her foot brushed against a patch of moss at the forest's edge, and she hesitated. Was it just her imagination? Or was there truly something waiting for her in the shadows?

"Elara!"

The voice startled her, pulling her from her thoughts. She turned to see Taren, one of the village's young hunters, jogging toward her. His dark hair was tied back in a messy knot, and his face was flushed from exertion.

"Elara, what are you doing?" he asked, his breath coming in short gasps. He glanced nervously at the forest behind her, his expression a mix of concern and disbelief. "You're not seriously thinking of going in there, are you?"

She smiled at him, though it was more out of habit than genuine amusement. Taren had always been one to worry about her, ever since they were children. He was kind, and there had been a time when they were younger that she had even considered him more than a friend. But now, his protectiveness only felt suffocating.

"I was just curious," Elara said, brushing a strand of hair behind her ear. "No need to sound the alarm."

Taren's eyes narrowed. "Curiosity doesn't belong anywhere near that place. You know what they say about the forest."

Elara sighed. "I've heard the stories, Taren. But don't you ever wonder what's really in there? What if it's not just old magic or curses? What if there's something more?"

Taren shook his head. "Elara, you're going to get yourself killed if you keep thinking like that. The forest is dangerous. You've heard about the creatures—wolves with glowing eyes, shadows that move on their own. It's not safe."

She turned back to the forest, her eyes scanning the trees. "Maybe. But I don't think it's as simple as danger and monsters. I think there's something in there—something that's been hidden for a long time."

Taren placed a hand on her shoulder, his touch gentle but firm. "Promise me you won't go in there."

For a moment, Elara considered making that promise. It would have been easy to agree and let the matter rest, to return to the village and continue living her life as she always had. But something in her heart, deep and unrelenting, refused to be silenced.

"I can't promise that," she said softly.

Taren's grip tightened, and he sighed in frustration. "Elara, please. Just be careful."

"I will," she replied, though she wasn't sure how much truth there was in her words.

With a final, lingering glance at the forest, Taren turned and began walking back toward the village. Elara watched him go, feeling a pang of guilt. He was only trying to protect her, but he didn't understand. No one in the village did. They didn't feel the pull of the forest the way she did. They didn't hear the whispers in the wind or see the strange lights in the darkness.

When Taren disappeared from view, Elara turned back to the forest. This time, she didn't hesitate.

The air inside the forest was different, cooler and heavier, as though it were infused with the very essence of the earth itself. The trees loomed overhead, their branches twisting and gnarled, blocking out much of the sunlight. A strange silence had fallen, and the only sounds were the soft crunch of leaves beneath Elara's boots and the occasional rustle of unseen creatures moving through the underbrush.

She walked cautiously, her senses alert to every movement and sound. The deeper she went, the more the world seemed to change around her. The air grew thicker, almost suffocating, and the light that filtered through the canopy took on a strange, greenish hue.

Despite the eerie atmosphere, Elara felt no fear. In fact, the further she ventured into the forest, the more she felt a strange sense of belonging. It was as though the forest was welcoming her, calling her home. The thought made her shiver, but it also filled her with a sense of purpose.

She didn't know how long she had been walking when she first noticed the carvings. At first, they were faint—symbols etched into the bark of the trees, so subtle that they could easily be mistaken for natural patterns in the wood. But as she moved deeper into the forest, the carvings became more distinct, more deliberate.

Elara stopped to examine one of the trees, running her fingers over the smooth lines of a symbol that had been carved deep into the bark. The symbol was unfamiliar to her, but it radiated a strange energy, as though it were alive. She traced the lines with her fingertips, feeling a faint warmth beneath the surface.

"What is this place?" she whispered to herself, her voice barely audible in the oppressive silence.

The forest gave no answer, but the wind stirred the leaves above her, carrying with it the faintest hint of a whisper. Elara's heart quickened. She had heard that sound before—the soft, unintelligible murmurs that seemed to come from nowhere and everywhere all at once.

She stepped back from the tree and continued walking, her pace quickening. The deeper she went, the more the forest seemed to change. The ground beneath her feet became soft and uneven, and strange plants grew in abundance—plants she had never seen before, with leaves that glowed faintly in the dim light. The air smelled different here, rich and earthy, with a hint of something sweet and unfamiliar.

Elara's pulse raced as she walked. She didn't know where she was going, but something deep inside her knew that she was on the right path. There was a purpose to her journey, even if she didn't fully understand it yet.

Then, she heard it.

At first, it was just a faint sound, barely noticeable over the rustling of the leaves. But as she moved closer, the sound grew louder, more distinct. It was a voice—a low, melodic voice, singing in a language she didn't recognize.

Elara followed the sound, her heart pounding in her chest. She pushed through the thick undergrowth, ignoring the branches that scratched at her skin and the roots that threatened to trip her. The voice called to her, and she couldn't help but follow.

Finally, she emerged into a clearing.

The sight that greeted her took her breath away.

In the center of the clearing stood an ancient tree, its trunk wide and gnarled, its branches stretching high into the sky. The tree was unlike any Elara had ever seen. Its bark was a deep, rich brown, and its leaves shimmered with an ethereal light, as though they were made of pure magic.

And beneath the tree stood a woman.

She was tall and slender, with long, silver hair that flowed down her back like a waterfall of moonlight. Her skin was pale and smooth, and her eyes—Elara couldn't tear her gaze away from her eyes. They were a deep, unnatural shade of violet, glowing with an inner light that seemed to pierce through Elara's very soul.

The woman's voice was the one Elara had heard, soft and melodic, singing a haunting melody that seemed to resonate with the very air around her. As Elara stepped into the clearing, the woman's song stopped, and she turned to face her.

For a long moment, neither of them spoke. Elara's breath caught in her throat as the woman's gaze settled on her, her violet eyes filled with an emotion Elara couldn't quite place—recognition? Curiosity? Fear?

"You came," the woman said, her voice soft and lilting, like the wind through the trees.

Elara blinked, confusion clouding her mind. "You were expecting me?"

The woman smiled, a sad, wistful smile that made Elara's heart ache. "In a way," she said. "You are not the first, though I had hoped you would not follow the path laid out for you."

Elara took a cautious step forward, her eyes never leaving the woman's face. "Who are you?"

The woman's smile faded, and her eyes grew distant, as though she were looking at something far beyond the clearing. "I am a keeper of secrets," she said. "A guardian of things that were lost long ago."

Elara frowned, her confusion growing. "What do you mean?"

The woman sighed, her gaze returning to Elara. "You are more than you know, Elara," she said, her voice filled with a quiet intensity. "The forest has called you for a reason."

Elara's heart skipped a beat at the sound of her name. "How do you know who I am?"

The woman didn't answer immediately. Instead, she stepped closer to Elara, her eyes searching her face as though she were looking for something hidden beneath the surface.

"You are part of something ancient," the woman said at last. "Something that has been in motion since long before you were born. The forest knows you, just as it knew those who came before you."

Elara's pulse quickened. "What are you talking about? What does the forest have to do with me?"

The woman reached out and placed a hand on Elara's shoulder, her touch warm and comforting. "You are the one the prophecy speaks of," she said, her voice barely above a whisper. "You are the child born under the blood moon."

Elara felt as though the ground had been ripped out from beneath her. The words echoed in her mind, but they didn't make sense. The prophecy? The blood moon? Those were just stories, myths passed down through generations. They couldn't possibly be real.

"I don't understand," Elara said, her voice shaking. "I'm just... I'm just me. I'm no one special."

The woman's gaze softened, and she gently squeezed Elara's shoulder. "You are more special than you realize," she said. "The Dark Queen fears you because she knows what you are capable of. You have the power to end her reign, to break the curse that binds her to the darkness."

Elara shook her head, disbelief flooding her. "No. That can't be true. I'm not a hero. I'm just... I'm just a girl from a village."

The woman smiled again, though this time there was a hint of sadness in her eyes. "Every hero begins as just a girl or a boy from a village," she said. "But destiny has a way of finding those who are meant for more."

Elara opened her mouth to protest, to deny the impossible truth that had been laid before her, but the words wouldn't come. Deep down, in a place she hadn't even known existed, she felt it—the connection, the pull of the prophecy. It had always been there, just beneath the surface, waiting for her to acknowledge it.

The woman stepped back, her hand falling away from Elara's shoulder. "You have a choice, Elara," she said. "You can turn away from this path, return to your village, and live your life as you always have. Or you can embrace your destiny and uncover the truth that lies within you."

Elara stood frozen in place, her mind racing. She had always felt different, always felt as though there was something more waiting for her beyond the boundaries of her village. But to be the one spoken of in the prophecy, to be the one destined to defeat the Dark Queen—that was something she had never imagined.

"I don't know if I can do this," Elara whispered, her voice filled with doubt.

The woman's violet eyes softened. "None of us know what we are capable of until we are tested," she said. "But the forest has chosen you, Elara. And I believe you are stronger than you know."

Elara looked down at the ground, her mind a whirlwind of emotions. She could feel the weight of the choice before her, the enormity of what it meant. To walk away would mean safety, but it would also mean living in ignorance of the truth. To accept her destiny would mean danger, but it would also mean discovering who she truly was.

After a long moment, Elara looked up, meeting the woman's gaze.

"I'll do it," she said, her voice steady. "I'll uncover the truth."

The woman smiled, a genuine smile this time, and nodded. "Then your journey begins."

As the woman's words faded into the air, the wind stirred the leaves of the ancient tree, and the clearing seemed to hum with a quiet energy. Elara took a deep breath, her heart racing, as she prepared to take her first step into the unknown.

The Forbidden Forest had called her, and now, there was no turning back.

Chapter 5: The Lost Sorcerer

The path through the Forbidden Forest was winding and treacherous, but Elara's steps were sure. She had spent days, possibly weeks, navigating the labyrinthine woods, her instincts sharpened by the cryptic wisdom of the forest guardian who had first set her on this journey. The farther she ventured, the more distant the village of Ashbourne felt—its small cottages and the comforting routine of village life now seemed like a memory from another lifetime.

Each night, Elara camped in secluded clearings, her mind filled with questions. She felt the weight of her destiny, and though the forest had revealed some of its secrets, it had not yet offered any clear answers. She still didn't fully understand the magnitude of the prophecy, or why she had been chosen to challenge the Dark Queen's reign. The guardian had said she possessed great power, but Elara had yet to feel anything like the magic the stories spoke of.

All she knew was that she had been called to find a sorcerer—an exiled figure who had once been one of the most powerful mages in Eldore. His name, or what little remained of it in the village's faded histories, was Theron. He had served the Dark Queen before she had come to power, before her transformation had turned her into the creature that now ruled the kingdom with fear and darkness. Theron had been cast out from her court, forced to live in hiding after he had dared to challenge her growing obsession with forbidden magic.

The rumors said that Theron had gone mad, that the years of exile had broken his mind and reduced him to a mere shadow of his former self. Others whispered that he had died long ago, his body claimed by the dark forces that now haunted the Forbidden Forest. Yet, Elara could feel his presence—somewhere deep within the woods, the lost sorcerer was waiting. She didn't know how she knew this, but the pull was undeniable.

The air grew colder as she ventured deeper into the heart of the forest, the trees towering overhead like sentinels guarding the ancient secrets of this place. A sense of unease gnawed at her, but Elara pressed on, her resolve unshaken.

By the time she reached a narrow ravine, the sun had begun to sink below the horizon, casting long shadows across the forest floor. Elara paused at the edge, her gaze sweeping across the rocky terrain below. A narrow stream trickled through the bottom of the ravine, but what drew her attention was the small, dilapidated cottage nestled between the rocks, almost hidden from view. Smoke rose lazily from its chimney, the only sign that someone still lived there.

Elara knew instinctively that this was Theron's dwelling. The sorcerer she had been seeking was here.

Taking a deep breath, she made her way down the rocky path, her heart pounding in her chest. As she approached the cottage, she felt a strange sensation in the air—an invisible force, like a web of magic, crackling just beneath the surface. It was unlike anything she had ever felt before, and it made the hairs on the back of her neck stand on end.

Elara reached the door and hesitated. She had no idea what to expect from Theron. Would he welcome her, or would he see her as a threat? What if the stories about his madness were true? She pushed the thoughts from her mind and steeled herself. She had come too far to turn back now.

She knocked on the door.

For a long moment, there was no response. Elara was about to knock again when the door creaked open, revealing a man who looked as though he had been carved from the very bones of the forest itself. He was tall and thin, his face gaunt and lined with age, his once-dark hair now streaked with gray. His eyes, however, were sharp and alert, glinting with a strange intensity that belied his worn appearance. He regarded Elara with a mixture of suspicion and curiosity, as if trying to discern whether she was friend or foe.

"What do you want?" he asked, his voice raspy and cold.

Elara swallowed hard, her mind racing for the right words. "I... I've come to find Theron," she said, her voice steady despite the nervousness she felt. "I need your help."

The man narrowed his eyes, studying her for a moment before stepping aside to let her enter. "You've found him," he said, his tone guarded. "But if you've come seeking help, you may find that you've wasted your time."

Elara stepped inside, her gaze sweeping over the interior of the cottage. It was as worn and weathered as its inhabitant. The walls were lined with dusty shelves filled with old, crumbling books and jars of strange herbs. A fire crackled weakly in the hearth, casting flickering shadows across the room. In the center of the cottage stood a small table, its surface cluttered with parchment, quills, and various arcane instruments.

Theron closed the door behind her and gestured for her to sit. Elara hesitated for a moment before taking a seat at the table. The sorcerer watched her closely, as though trying to decide whether she was a threat or merely a curiosity.

"So," he said after a long pause, "you've come seeking the help of a broken old man. What could possibly bring someone like you here?"

Elara met his gaze, her voice firm. "I was told that you know the truth about the Dark Queen—about the magic that binds her to the throne. I need to know how to stop her."

Theron's eyes darkened, and for a moment, Elara thought she had said the wrong thing. His jaw tightened, and he turned away from her, pacing the length of the cottage as if wrestling with some internal battle.

"You don't know what you're asking," he muttered, more to himself than to her.

"I know the risks," Elara said, her voice steady. "But I have no choice. There's a prophecy—"

Theron stopped in his tracks and turned to face her, his eyes narrowing. "The prophecy," he interrupted, his voice dripping with disdain. "Yes, I've heard of it. The child born under the blood moon, destined to break the Queen's curse. You're the one, aren't you? The Cursed Child."

Elara nodded, unsure of how to respond to the bitterness in his voice.

Theron let out a bitter laugh. "I should have known," he said, shaking his head. "The forest wouldn't have let you find me otherwise."

He turned away again, his hands gripping the back of a chair as though he were trying to steady himself. "Do you have any idea what you're up against?" he asked, his voice low. "The Dark Queen isn't just some tyrant. She's bound to forces far older and far darker than you could possibly imagine. Her power is not her own—it's a gift, if you can call it that, from the ancient ones who rule the shadows. The same magic that sustains her will destroy anyone who tries to take it from her."

Elara frowned. "Then there must be a way to break the curse," she said, her mind racing. "You were once close to her. You must know something."

Theron laughed again, though this time there was no humor in it. "Close to her? Yes, I was once a part of her court, back when she was still Morgana—before she became the Dark Queen." His voice softened slightly as he spoke the name, as if it pained him to remember the woman Morgana had once been. "But that was a long time ago. I warned her not to delve into the forbidden magic, not to make the pact with the ancient ones. But she wouldn't listen. She was consumed by her hunger for power, and now... now she is bound to that power for eternity."

Elara leaned forward, her eyes searching his face. "But if there's a curse, there has to be a way to break it. What is she bound to?"

Theron's eyes flicked toward the fire, the flames reflecting in their dark depths. "The pact she made," he said slowly, "was not just a simple exchange of power. It was a binding—a merging of her soul with the ancient ones who dwell beyond the veil of this world. They granted her the power she craved, but in return, she is tied to them. She cannot die, not as long as the pact holds. And neither can her rule be ended."

Elara's heart sank. "So it's impossible."

Theron shook his head. "Not impossible. But difficult. The key to breaking the pact lies in the very magic that binds her. The forbidden spells that she used to create the pact are the same ones that can unravel it. But those spells are dangerous—more dangerous than you can imagine."

Elara's mind raced, her thoughts swirling with the enormity of what Theron was saying. The Dark Queen was bound to the very forces of darkness that had corrupted her, and the only way to break the curse was to use the same forbidden magic that had been her undoing. It was a dangerous path, but if there was even a chance of ending Morgana's reign, Elara knew she had to take it.

"I'm willing to learn," she said, her voice steady. "Teach me the spells."

Theron's gaze hardened, and he turned to face her fully, his expression unreadable. "You don't know what you're asking," he said. "The magic you seek isn't just dangerous—it's corrupting. It will change you, just as it changed Morgana. Once you begin down that path, there's no turning back."

Elara held his gaze, her resolve unshaken. "I have no choice," she said. "If I don't stop her, no one will."

Theron studied her for a long moment, as if searching for any hint of doubt. When he found none, he sighed heavily and sat down at the table across from her. "Very well," he said, his voice low. "I will teach you. But know this: once you begin, you will be bound to the magic, just as Morgana is. The power will come at a cost."

Elara nodded. "I understand."

Theron's expression softened slightly, and for the first time since she had entered the cottage, Elara saw a flicker of something in his eyes—respect, perhaps, or admiration for her courage.

"Then we begin now," he said.

The next few days passed in a blur of intense study and practice. Theron proved to be a harsh and exacting teacher, his patience thin and his expectations high. Elara quickly learned that magic was not simply a matter of incantations and gestures—it required focus, discipline, and an understanding of the forces that governed the natural world.

Theron taught her the basics first—the manipulation of energy, the weaving of simple spells to bend light and shadow. But it wasn't long before he introduced her to the forbidden magic, the dark spells that had been outlawed for centuries. These were the spells that Morgana had used to bind herself to the ancient ones, the spells that had the power to break the curse but also the power to corrupt those who wielded them.

The magic was unlike anything Elara had ever imagined. It wasn't just a tool—it was a living force, a dark and seductive presence that whispered in her mind, promising power and control. She could feel it creeping into her soul, tempting her to give in to its allure. But each time she felt herself slipping, she reminded herself of her purpose. She wasn't doing this for herself—she was doing it to stop Morgana, to save Eldore from the darkness that had consumed it.

Theron watched her closely, his eyes never leaving her as she practiced the spells. He corrected her mistakes with sharp words and stern looks, but there was something else in his gaze—something that suggested he wasn't just teaching her magic. He was testing her, gauging her strength and her willpower, waiting to see if she would falter.

One evening, as they sat by the fire after a long day of practice, Elara asked him a question that had been weighing on her mind.

"Why did you stay here?" she asked, her voice soft. "Why didn't you leave the forest after Morgana exiled you?"

Theron's expression darkened, and for a moment, Elara thought he wouldn't answer. But then he sighed and leaned back in his chair, his gaze distant.

"Because I couldn't leave," he said, his voice heavy with regret. "I was bound to her, just as she is bound to the ancient ones. The magic we practiced together—it created a bond between us, a bond that can't be broken."

Elara frowned. "But you're not like her. You didn't follow her down that path."

Theron's gaze flicked toward the fire, and his jaw tightened. "No," he said softly. "But that doesn't mean I'm free from the consequences."

Elara didn't press him further. She could sense that there was more to Theron's story, more to his connection to Morgana than he was willing to reveal. But for now, it was enough to know that he had once been close to her, that he had once shared in her power.

As the days passed, Elara's mastery of the dark magic grew. She could feel its power coursing through her veins, and though it frightened her, it also exhilarated her. She was stronger now, more capable than she had ever been before. But with that strength came a growing unease—a sense that the magic was changing her, just as Theron had warned.

She began to hear whispers in her dreams, voices that spoke in the same ancient language she had heard in the forest. They called to her, urging her to embrace the full extent of her power, to give herself over to the darkness. Each morning, she woke with a sense of dread, the whispers still echoing in her mind.

But despite the growing darkness within her, Elara refused to give in. She had come too far to turn back now.

One night, as they sat by the fire, Theron spoke words that sent a chill through her heart.

"The time has come," he said, his voice quiet but filled with a grim certainty. "You are ready."

Elara met his gaze, her heart pounding in her chest. She knew what he meant. The time had come for her to face the Dark Queen, to challenge the curse that bound her to the throne.

But as she looked into Theron's eyes, she couldn't shake the feeling that there was more to his words than simple instruction. He was afraid—for her, perhaps, or for what she might become.

"You must be careful," Theron said, his voice low. "The Dark Queen's power is greater than you can imagine. And if you're not careful, you could end up just like her."

Elara nodded, though the weight of his warning hung heavily in the air. She was ready, but the path ahead was more dangerous than she had ever imagined.

As dawn broke the next morning, Elara stood at the edge of the forest, her heart filled with both determination and fear. She had learned much from Theron, but now it was up to her. The Dark Queen awaited, and with her, the fate of Eldore.

Elara took a deep breath and stepped into the shadows, the magic she had learned swirling within her like a storm.

Her journey had only just begun.

Chapter 6: The Quest for the Ancient Relics

Elara stood in the dim light of the forest, her mind reeling with the weight of what Theron had revealed. Breaking the Dark Queen's curse wasn't just a matter of defeating her in battle or undoing her forbidden spells. The curse that bound Morgana to the ancient forces of darkness was woven into the very fabric of her soul. To unravel it, Elara needed more than magic—she needed the ancient relics of power that had been scattered across Eldore long before Morgana's reign.

There were three of them, each hidden in a place so treacherous that only the most desperate or foolhardy would dare to seek them. Legends spoke of their immense power, artifacts from a time when the ancient gods themselves walked the earth. Each relic was said to hold a fragment of the divine, and together, they formed the key to breaking the most powerful of curses. But retrieving them would be no easy task.

The first relic, according to Theron, lay in the depths of a haunted mountain known as Dur'Garran. It was a place shrouded in legend, its peak often obscured by dark clouds that never lifted. Few who ventured into its depths ever returned, and those who did spoke of spirits that haunted the twisting caverns, their voices echoing through the stone like the whispers of the damned. The mountain was said to be alive with dangerous magic, its very core imbued with the remnants of a battle fought long ago between the gods and an ancient, vengeful race of creatures.

Elara knew that this was where her quest must begin. She had no other choice. Morgana's power grew stronger with each passing day, and if Elara didn't act soon, the entire kingdom would be lost to the darkness. The relics were her only hope.

The journey to Dur'Garran was long and perilous. Elara traveled alone, her thoughts consumed by the enormity of the task ahead. The forest eventually gave way to open plains, and the rolling hills soon turned to jagged cliffs and rocky outcrops as she neared the mountain range. As she approached the foot of the haunted mountain, a sense of dread began to settle over her.

The air around Dur'Garran was thick with an unnatural chill, the sky perpetually gray, as though the sun itself dared not shine upon the mountain. Jagged peaks rose high above her, their summits lost in the swirling mists. The entrance to the caverns lay before her, a gaping maw in the side of the mountain that seemed to beckon her forward.

Elara hesitated at the threshold, her heart pounding in her chest. She had faced many dangers already—her encounters with the forbidden magic, the creatures of the forest, and the ominous power of the Dark Queen herself—but this felt different. This place wasn't just dangerous; it was cursed. Every instinct in her body screamed at her to turn back, to find another way. But there was no other way.

Taking a deep breath, Elara stepped into the darkness.

The air inside the mountain was cold and stale, and Elara's footsteps echoed unnervingly in the stillness. The path before her was narrow, the walls of the cavern closing in around her as she descended deeper into the mountain's heart. The only light came from the faint glow of the crystals embedded in the rock, casting eerie shadows that seemed to shift and move as she passed.

Theron had told her of the dangers that lurked within Dur'Garran, but nothing could have prepared her for the oppressive atmosphere of the place. It felt as though the mountain itself was alive, watching her every move, waiting for her to make a mistake. The deeper she went, the heavier the air became, until it felt as though she were walking through water.

After what felt like hours of walking, the narrow tunnel opened up into a vast cavern, its ceiling so high that Elara couldn't see the top. Massive stone pillars lined the walls, their surfaces etched with runes that glowed faintly in the dim light. At the center of the cavern stood an altar, its surface covered in dust and cobwebs. And upon that altar lay the first relic—a small, intricately carved orb that pulsed with a faint, otherworldly light.

Elara's heart leapt at the sight of it. She had found the first relic.

But as she took a step toward the altar, a deep rumble echoed through the cavern, and the ground beneath her feet trembled. She froze, her hand instinctively reaching for the dagger at her belt.

Out of the shadows, a figure emerged—a creature unlike anything Elara had ever seen. It stood on two legs, its body massive and hunched, covered in thick, matted fur. Its eyes glowed with an unnatural light, and its claws, long and razor-sharp, scraped against the stone as it moved toward her. The air around it shimmered with magic, and Elara could feel the weight of its presence pressing down on her.

The creature let out a low growl, its breath hot and rancid as it bared its teeth. Elara took a step back, her mind racing. She had no idea what this creature was, but it was clear that it was guarding the relic. And it wasn't going to let her take it without a fight.

Elara's hand tightened around the hilt of her dagger as the creature advanced, its eyes locked on her with a predatory intensity. She had no choice but to fight.

The creature lunged at her with a speed that belied its massive size, its claws slashing through the air. Elara barely had time to react, diving to the side just as the creature's claws raked the stone where she had been standing. She rolled to her feet, her dagger flashing in the dim light as she slashed at the creature's side. The blade barely grazed its thick fur, and the creature let out a roar of anger, swiping at her with its massive paw.

Elara ducked under the blow, her mind racing. Her dagger was useless against this thing's hide. She needed to find another way to defeat it, and fast. As she dodged another swipe, her gaze fell on the glowing runes etched into the pillars around the cavern. The air around them shimmered with magic, and Elara realized that they were more than just decoration—they were part of an ancient spell.

The creature lunged at her again, and Elara barely managed to leap out of its path. She had to buy herself some time.

Taking a deep breath, Elara focused her mind, drawing on the magic that Theron had taught her. She could feel the dark energy swirling around her, seductive and dangerous, but she pushed the temptation aside. She wasn't using this power for herself—she was using it to survive.

With a flick of her wrist, Elara sent a bolt of magic toward the nearest pillar, her heart pounding as the energy connected with the glowing runes. The pillar vibrated, and the runes flared to life, sending a shockwave through the cavern. The creature let out a howl of pain, its massive body convulsing as the magic surged through it.

Elara didn't hesitate. She sprinted toward the next pillar, sending another bolt of magic toward the runes. The pillar flared to life, and another shockwave rippled through the cavern. The creature staggered, its eyes glowing with fury as it struggled to maintain its footing.

But Elara could see the magic taking its toll on the beast. The runes were weakening it, draining its strength. She just needed to keep going.

She darted to the next pillar, her hands trembling as she sent another bolt of magic toward the runes. The air crackled with energy, and the creature let out a final, agonized roar before collapsing to the ground, its massive body lifeless.

Elara stood frozen for a moment, her chest heaving as she caught her breath. The cavern was silent once more, the only sound the faint hum of the magic still lingering in the air.

Slowly, she made her way to the altar, her legs trembling with exhaustion. The orb lay before her, its surface smooth and cool to the touch. As her fingers closed around it, a surge of energy rushed through her, filling her with a sense of power and purpose. This was the first relic, the key to breaking the Dark Queen's curse.

But even as she held the relic in her hands, Elara knew that her journey was far from over. There were still two more relics to find, each hidden in places just as dangerous—perhaps even more so—than Dur'Garran. And the Dark Queen would not sit idly by as Elara gathered the means to destroy her.

With the relic safely tucked into her satchel, Elara turned and made her way back through the winding tunnels of the mountain, her mind already racing with thoughts of the next leg of her quest.

The second relic lay in the depths of the Emerald Marshes, a place known for its deadly terrain and the creatures that lurked beneath its murky waters. Legends told of a great serpent that guarded the relic, a creature born of the marsh's magic and bound to protect it at all costs. Elara had heard stories of travelers who had ventured into the marshes, never to return. But she had no choice. The relics were her only hope.

The journey to the marshes was long and grueling. Elara traveled day and night, her only companions the endless horizon and the weight of the relic she had already recovered. The closer she got to the marshes, the more desolate the land became. The trees thinned, giving way to wide expanses of stagnant water and dense, tangled vines. The air was thick with the smell of decay, and the ground squelched beneath her boots as she made her way deeper into the swamp.

Elara moved cautiously, her senses alert for any sign of danger. The marshes were known for their treacherous terrain, and the waters were said to be home to all manner of deadly creatures. She could feel the weight of the magic in the air, thick and oppressive, as though the marsh itself was alive and watching her every move.

As she waded through the murky waters, Elara couldn't shake the feeling that something was watching her. She stopped, her hand resting on the hilt of her dagger, her eyes scanning the dense foliage around her. The marsh was eerily silent, the only sound the faint ripple of water as it lapped against the reeds.

Then, without warning, the water exploded in front of her.

A massive serpent, its scales gleaming with a sickly green light, erupted from the marsh, its jaws wide as it lunged toward her. Elara barely had time to react, diving to the side as the creature's fangs snapped shut just inches from her face. She scrambled to her feet, her heart pounding as she drew her dagger.

The serpent coiled around her, its body massive and sinuous, its eyes glowing with an unnatural light. Elara could feel the magic radiating from the creature, ancient and powerful. This was the guardian of the second relic, and it wasn't going to let her take it without a fight.

Elara's mind raced as the serpent lunged at her again, its massive body crashing through the water with incredible force. She dodged its attack, slashing at its side with her dagger, but the blade barely made a scratch on its thick scales. The creature hissed in anger, its body coiling around her as it prepared to strike again.

She couldn't defeat it with brute force—she needed to think. As the serpent lunged at her once more, Elara dodged to the side, her eyes scanning the marsh for anything she could use to her advantage. Then she saw it—a cluster of glowing plants growing along the edge of the water, their leaves pulsing with a faint, otherworldly light. Elara recognized them immediately. They were the source of the marsh's magic.

Without hesitation, Elara sprinted toward the plants, the serpent hot on her heels. She grabbed a handful of the glowing leaves, their magic surging through her as she crushed them in her hands. The serpent lunged at her again, but this time, Elara was ready. She hurled the crushed leaves at the creature, the magic crackling in the air as the serpent let out a deafening hiss of pain.

The creature writhed in agony, its body thrashing in the water as the magic took hold. Elara didn't waste any time. She sprinted toward the center of the marsh, where the second relic lay hidden beneath a tangled mass of roots and vines. Her hands shook as she pulled the relic free, its surface slick with mud and water.

The serpent let out one final, anguished hiss before collapsing into the water, its body disappearing beneath the murky depths.

Elara stood frozen for a moment, her breath coming in ragged gasps as she clutched the second relic to her chest. The marsh was silent once more, the only sound the faint ripple of water as it lapped against the shore.

She had done it. She had recovered the second relic.

But as Elara stood in the silence of the marsh, she couldn't shake the feeling that the real danger had yet to come. There was still one more relic to find, and with each step she took, the Dark Queen's power grew stronger.

The third and final relic was hidden deep within the Valley of Shadows, a place so remote and dangerous that even the bravest warriors refused to venture there. It was said that the valley was home to the spirits of the dead, their souls trapped in the eternal twilight that blanketed the land. The air itself was thick with magic, and those who entered the valley often found themselves lost in the mists, their minds twisted by the darkness.

Elara had no choice. The third relic was the final key to breaking Morgana's curse, and without it, her quest would be for nothing.

The journey to the Valley of Shadows was the hardest yet. Elara's body ached with exhaustion, her mind weighed down by the constant pressure of the magic she carried. The relics pulsed with power, their presence a constant reminder of the enormous task that lay before her.

When she finally reached the valley, Elara understood why so few had returned from its depths. The landscape was barren and lifeless, the sky a perpetual shade of gray. A thick mist clung to the ground, swirling around her feet as she made her way deeper into the valley. The air was heavy with the stench of death, and Elara could feel the weight of the spirits that lingered in the shadows, watching her with cold, hungry eyes.

She moved cautiously, her hand never leaving the hilt of her dagger. The valley was silent, save for the occasional whisper of wind that seemed to carry the voices of the dead. Elara's pulse quickened as she felt the magic of the third relic calling to her, pulling her deeper into the heart of the valley.

After what felt like hours of walking, she reached a small, stone shrine nestled in the center of the valley. The third relic lay before her, its surface gleaming with a faint, ethereal light.

Elara reached out to take the relic, but as her fingers brushed against it, a cold voice echoed through the valley.

"You dare to take what is not yours."

Elara spun around, her heart racing as a figure stepped out of the mist. The figure was tall and cloaked in shadow, its face obscured by darkness. But Elara could feel the power radiating from it—the same power that had bound Morgana to the throne.

This was no ordinary spirit.

"I have no choice," Elara said, her voice steady despite the fear that gnawed at her. "I need the relic to stop the Dark Queen."

The figure let out a low, menacing laugh. "The relics belong to the ancient ones," it said, its voice like ice. "And you are not worthy to claim them."

Elara's hand tightened around the hilt of her dagger. She had come too far to fail now.

"I will stop her," she said, her voice filled with determination. "No matter what it takes."

The figure stepped forward, its eyes glowing with an eerie light. "Then prove yourself," it said.

And with those words, the valley erupted into chaos.

The battle was fierce and unrelenting, the figure moving with the speed and precision of a predator as it attacked Elara from all sides. She dodged and parried, her mind racing as she fought to keep up with the spirit's onslaught. The magic of the relics pulsed in her chest, filling her with a sense of power and purpose, but it wasn't enough. The spirit was too strong, its attacks too precise.

Elara's strength was fading, her body growing weak from the constant strain of the fight. She knew she couldn't keep this up much longer.

In a moment of desperation, Elara reached deep within herself, drawing on the dark magic that Theron had taught her. The forbidden power surged through her veins, filling her with a sense of strength and fury that she had never felt before. She could feel the darkness creeping into her soul, tempting her to give in, but she pushed it aside.

With a final, desperate cry, Elara unleashed a torrent of magic, the energy crackling through the air as it slammed into the figure. The spirit let out a scream of agony before disintegrating into the mist, its presence vanishing from the valley.

Elara collapsed to the ground, her breath coming in ragged gasps as the weight of the battle finally caught up with her.

She had won.

Slowly, she pushed herself to her feet and made her way back to the shrine. The third relic pulsed with power, its surface cool to the touch as Elara took it in her hands.

She had done it. She had gathered all three relics.

But as she stood in the eerie silence of the Valley of Shadows, Elara couldn't shake the feeling that the real battle had yet to come.

Morgana was waiting, and with each relic Elara gathered, the Dark Queen's power grew stronger.

Her journey was far from over.

Chapter 7: The Guardian of the Mountain

The mountain loomed before Elara, its jagged peaks piercing the storm-laden sky like the talons of some ancient, slumbering beast. Dur'Garran, the haunted mountain, had a reputation that stretched across the kingdom of Eldore. Its dark legends spoke of those who had entered its depths seeking glory or treasure, only to be swallowed by the mountain's endless maze of caverns and never seen again. It was a place where the past clung to every stone, and the whispers of long-forgotten spirits echoed in the biting wind. But within its heart lay the first relic, the key to breaking Morgana's curse.

Elara stood at the foot of the mountain, her cloak drawn tightly around her to shield her from the cold wind. The air was thick with a sense of foreboding, and the path ahead felt more treacherous with every step she took. Yet, despite the fear gnawing at the edges of her resolve, she knew she could not turn back. The weight of her destiny pressed heavily on her shoulders, and the lives of countless innocents hung in the balance.

She glanced at the narrow path that wound up the mountain, disappearing into the thick mist that clung to its slopes. Somewhere within lay the Guardian of Dur'Garran, the spirit tasked with protecting the relic. Elara didn't know what form the Guardian would take, but the stories told of a creature bound by ancient magic, its very existence tied to the relic it protected. It would not give up its charge easily.

Taking a deep breath, Elara began the ascent.

The climb was grueling. The rocky path was slick with moisture from the perpetual mist, and the air grew thinner as Elara made her way higher. Her muscles ached, and the cold bit at her skin, but she pressed on, each step taking her closer to the relic. As she climbed, the mountain seemed to close in around her. The mist thickened, obscuring her vision, and the wind howled through the crags, carrying with it faint whispers that sent chills down her spine.

Elara paused for a moment to catch her breath, her heart pounding in her chest. She wiped a hand across her brow, brushing away the beads of sweat that had formed despite the cold. Her thoughts drifted to Theron, the exiled sorcerer who had reluctantly become her mentor. His teachings had been harsh but necessary, and his warnings about the dangers she would face had been clear.

"The Guardian is not just a beast to be slain," Theron had told her the night before she left for the mountain. "It is a test—a force of nature bound by ancient magic. You will not defeat it through strength alone. It will test every part of you: your courage, your wisdom, and your will. If you falter, it will devour you."

Elara had nodded, though doubt had gnawed at her. She had trained hard with Theron, learning the ways of magic and honing her skills, but was she truly prepared to face such a challenge? She had never faced a creature as powerful as the Guardian. Would her strength be enough?

Pushing the doubts aside, she continued upward, her boots scraping against the loose gravel of the mountain path. Hours passed, though it felt like days, and the mist grew thicker still, swirling around her like a living thing. The path narrowed to a razor-thin ledge, and Elara's heart raced as she carefully placed one foot in front of the other, her arms outstretched to keep her balance.

Suddenly, the mist parted.

Elara stepped onto a wide plateau that stretched out before her, the ground littered with jagged stones and the remnants of ancient ruins. Massive pillars of rock jutted up from the earth, their surfaces etched with strange runes that pulsed faintly with a soft, blue light. At the far end of the plateau stood a stone altar, and upon it rested a small, glowing orb—the first relic.

But Elara's eyes were drawn not to the relic, but to the figure standing before it.

The Guardian.

It was a creature of pure magic, its form shifting and changing as though it were made of mist and shadow. One moment, it appeared as a towering, humanoid figure, its body composed of swirling energy; the next, it dissolved into a cloud of ethereal light. Its eyes, glowing with an otherworldly blue hue, were locked onto Elara, and she could feel the weight of its gaze pressing down on her.

For a long moment, neither of them moved. Elara's heart raced, her mind screaming at her to run, but she stood her ground. She had come too far to back down now.

The Guardian spoke, its voice a deep, resonant echo that seemed to come from all around her.

"You have come seeking the relic," it said, its tone both calm and menacing. "But to claim it, you must prove yourself worthy. The relic is not meant for the weak or the foolish. Only those with the strength to face their darkest fears may take it."

Elara swallowed hard, her mouth dry. "I am not weak," she said, her voice steady despite the fear clawing at her insides. "I have come to break the curse that binds this kingdom. The relic is the key to that."

The Guardian's eyes flared with intensity. "Then face the trials, Elara of Ashbourne. Only by passing through the fire of your own soul will you be deemed worthy."

Without warning, the Guardian raised its hand, and the ground beneath Elara's feet shifted. The stones rippled like water, and the world around her began to blur. She felt herself being pulled into a vortex of light and shadow, her body spinning as reality itself seemed to unravel.

When the world finally settled, Elara found herself standing in a dark, unfamiliar landscape. The air was thick with tension, and the ground beneath her was uneven, like the surface of a barren wasteland. In the distance, jagged mountains rose against a blood-red sky, their peaks obscured by swirling clouds of black smoke.

She was no longer on Dur'Garran.

Elara's heart raced as she tried to make sense of her surroundings. Where was she? Had the Guardian transported her to another realm? Was this some kind of illusion?

A voice echoed in her mind, the Guardian's voice, but softer now, more distant. "The first trial is that of courage. Face the darkness that lies within you, or be consumed by it."

Elara turned, her eyes scanning the desolate landscape. She had no idea what form the trial would take, but she knew it would not be easy. The air was heavy with a sense of foreboding, and every instinct told her that something was coming.

Then, out of the shadows, they appeared.

Figures, shrouded in black, their faces hidden beneath hoods. They moved silently, their steps eerily synchronized as they approached her. There were dozens of them, their forms shifting and flickering as though they were made of smoke.

Elara's hand went to her dagger, but something told her that these were not enemies she could fight with steel. The figures stopped a few feet away, forming a loose circle around her. Their presence was oppressive, and Elara could feel their eyes—though hidden—boring into her.

One of the figures stepped forward, its voice a low hiss. "You are nothing, Elara. A child playing at hero. You are weak, and you will fail."

Another figure joined in. "You are not worthy of the power you seek. You will be consumed by it, just as Morgana was."

Elara clenched her fists, her heart pounding. The figures circled closer, their voices growing louder, more insistent.

"You will die here, alone, forgotten."

"You will never defeat the Dark Queen."

"You are a fool to think you can succeed."

The voices echoed in her mind, each one a dagger of doubt and fear. Elara tried to block them out, but they pressed in on her from all sides, their words cutting deeper and deeper into her soul. She could feel her resolve wavering, her strength faltering. The weight of their accusations was overwhelming, and for a moment, she believed them.

What if they were right?

What if she was nothing more than a foolish girl from a forgotten village? What if she had overestimated her abilities, and the Dark Queen was destined to win?

The voices grew louder, a cacophony of despair and doubt that threatened to drown her.

But then, through the storm of voices, another memory surfaced—a voice, strong and clear, cutting through the darkness.

Theron.

"You are stronger than you know," he had told her. "The magic you wield is dangerous, yes, but it is also a part of you. Trust in yourself, Elara. You have the strength to overcome whatever lies ahead."

Elara took a deep breath, her grip on her dagger tightening. The voices still clawed at her, but she refused to give in. She wasn't just some weak, helpless girl. She had faced dangers before, and she had come out stronger because of them. She wasn't going to let these shadows break her.

"I am not weak," Elara said, her voice steady and filled with conviction. "I have come too far to give up now. I may be afraid, but I will not let that fear control me."

The figures hesitated, their whispers faltering.

"I will not be consumed by doubt," she continued, stepping forward to meet their gaze. "I will not be consumed by the darkness. I will face whatever comes, and I will win."

The figures recoiled, their forms flickering like candles in the wind. One by one, they dissolved into the

shadows, their voices fading into the distance.

Elara stood alone in the desolate landscape, her heart still racing, but her mind clear. The trial of courage had tested her in ways she had not expected, but she had faced it, and she had won.

The world around her shifted again, and Elara found herself back on the plateau, the Guardian watching her with unreadable eyes.

"You have passed the trial of courage," it said, its voice filled with a strange mix of approval and caution. "But there are still two more trials to face."

Elara nodded, her pulse still quickened from the first trial. She knew that the challenges ahead would only grow more difficult, but she was ready. She had to be.

THE SECOND TRIAL CAME swiftly. The world around her blurred once more, and Elara found herself standing in a vast, open field. The sun hung low in the sky, casting long shadows across the golden grass. It was a peaceful scene, almost idyllic, but Elara knew better than to trust the surface.

"The trial of wisdom," the Guardian's voice echoed in her mind. "You must navigate the path before you, but choose wisely. A single misstep, and all will be lost."

Elara frowned, scanning the field. It looked harmless enough, but she could feel the magic at work, twisting the landscape in ways she couldn't yet see. The grass seemed to ripple like water, and the shadows cast by the setting sun seemed to shift and dance as though they were alive.

In the distance, she could see several paths leading out of the field, each one stretching toward the horizon. They all looked identical, but Elara knew that only one would lead her to the relic. The others would lead her to ruin.

She took a deep breath, her mind racing as she tried to make sense of the puzzle before her. There had to be a clue, something that would guide her in the right direction. But the field was vast, and the paths indistinguishable from one another.

"Think, Elara," she whispered to herself. "Use what you've learned."

Theron had taught her that magic wasn't just about power—it was about understanding the forces at play, about seeing the patterns that others missed. Elara closed her eyes, reaching out with her senses, trying to feel the flow of magic in the air.

At first, there was nothing. The field was silent, still.

But then, she felt it—a faint pulse, like the beating of a distant heart. It was subtle, almost imperceptible, but it was there. The magic was flowing, and if she could follow it, it would lead her to the right path.

Elara opened her eyes, her focus sharpened. She stepped forward, letting the magic guide her, her feet carrying her toward one of the paths. The pulse grew stronger as she neared it, and Elara felt a surge of confidence. This was the right way.

But as she took her first step onto the path, the ground beneath her feet shifted, and the world spun around her.

She was falling.

The ground rushed up to meet her, and Elara braced herself for the impact. But it never came. Instead, she found herself standing once more on the plateau, her body trembling with the residual magic of the trial.

"You chose poorly," the Guardian's voice boomed, its tone filled with cold judgment. "The trial of wisdom is not about following instinct alone. It is about understanding the consequences of every decision."

Elara's heart sank, the weight of her failure pressing down on her. She had been so sure of her choice, but she had been wrong. The realization stung, but she knew that she couldn't let it break her.

"I will not fail again," she said, her voice filled with determination.

The Guardian regarded her for a long moment before nodding. "Then face the final trial."

THE THIRD AND FINAL trial was unlike anything Elara had experienced before.

The world around her dissolved, and she found herself standing in a dark, endless void. There was no sound, no light, no sense of time. She was alone, floating in the abyss, her mind struggling to comprehend the emptiness around her.

"The trial of resolve," the Guardian's voice whispered in her mind. "The greatest test of all."

Elara's heart pounded in her chest as the void closed in around her. There was no way out, no path to follow. The darkness pressed against her, suffocating her, and for the first time, Elara felt truly helpless.

But she refused to give in.

She closed her eyes, focusing on the one thing that had carried her through every challenge, every hardship: her will to fight. She wasn't just doing this for herself. She was doing it for the people of Eldore, for the lives that Morgana had destroyed, for the kingdom that had been torn apart by darkness.

"I will not be broken," Elara whispered, her voice filled with quiet strength.

The void seemed to tremble around her, as though the very fabric of reality was reacting to her words. Elara could feel the darkness pushing against her, trying to crush her spirit, but she stood firm. She would not be defeated.

Slowly, the void began to recede, the darkness peeling away like mist. Light broke through the shadows, and Elara felt the weight of the trial lift from her shoulders.

When the world settled once more, she found herself back on the plateau, the Guardian standing before her, its eyes glowing with a strange, ancient light.

"You have passed the trials," it said, its voice filled with reverence. "You have proven yourself worthy of the relic."

The Guardian stepped aside, revealing the stone altar and the glowing orb that rested upon it.

Elara approached the altar, her heart pounding as she reached out to take the relic. The moment her fingers touched the smooth surface of the orb, a surge of energy rushed through her, filling her with a sense of power and purpose. This was the first relic, the key to breaking Morgana's curse.

But as Elara stood on the plateau, the relic pulsing in her hands, she couldn't shake the feeling that her journey had only just begun.

The Dark Queen was waiting, and with each step Elara took, the path ahead grew darker.

Her courage, wisdom, and resolve had been tested, but the greatest challenge was still to come.

Chapter 8: The Dark Queen's Wrath

The air around Elara grew colder, the wind biting through her cloak as she descended from Dur'Garran with the first relic in hand. The pulse of its magic throbbed softly in her palm, its power both a comfort and a reminder of the dangerous journey that still lay ahead. She had passed the trials of the Guardian and claimed the relic, but she knew that her true battle had only just begun. With each step, the weight of her destiny pressed down on her more heavily. And as much as she tried to shake the feeling, Elara couldn't escape the gnawing sense that something dark was closing in on her.

Her thoughts drifted back to Morgana—the Dark Queen who had once been her aunt, but now was something far more monstrous. Morgana's corruption had twisted her into a creature of darkness, bound by forbidden magic to the throne. Elara had always known that eventually, Morgana would learn of her quest to break the curse. But the looming sense of dread told her that Morgana already knew.

The relic in Elara's satchel seemed to hum in response, as if resonating with the dark magic that lurked on the edge of her awareness. The wind howled through the craggy peaks of the mountain, and Elara quickened her pace, her eyes scanning the path ahead for any sign of danger.

She was not alone.

Far to the north, in the shadowed heart of Eldore, the Dark Queen sat upon her throne. Her once-beautiful face was now a mask of malevolent power, her eyes glowing with an eerie light as she gazed into the swirling depths of a dark mirror. The mirror showed her many things: the rise and fall of kingdoms, the whispers of treachery among her enemies, and, most importantly, the movements of those who sought to challenge her rule.

It was in this mirror that Morgana had first seen Elara.

The prophecy of the Cursed Child had been a distant worry for many years—an old tale, whispered by superstitious villagers, one that Morgana had long dismissed. But now, as she watched Elara in the mirror, the truth of the prophecy burned in her heart like a cold fire. Elara had the relic. She was gathering the tools that could break the curse and end Morgana's reign.

The Dark Queen's lips curled into a cruel smile. She would not allow it.

With a flick of her wrist, Morgana waved her hand over the mirror, her fingers tracing intricate patterns in the air. The surface of the mirror rippled, and the image of Elara vanished, replaced by the dark, swirling shadows that always danced just beyond the edges of Morgana's perception.

Her minions.

The shadows, born of the same forbidden magic that sustained Morgana, were her most loyal servants. They had no form of their own, only the twisted, writhing shapes of darkness that responded to their queen's will. They lived in the shadows, moving through the world unseen, waiting for the moment to strike.

Morgana's eyes blazed with fury as she called them forth.

"Find her," she whispered, her voice like the hiss of a serpent. "Find Elara and bring me her heart."

The shadows moved at once, slipping through the walls of the throne room like smoke, spreading out across the kingdom to hunt their prey. Morgana watched them go, her smile widening as she imagined the look of terror on Elara's face when they finally found her.

The Dark Queen's wrath had been unleashed.

ELARA COULD FEEL THE shift in the air long before she saw anything. There was a thickness to it, a sense of something lurking just out of sight. The sky had darkened unnaturally, the mist swirling in strange, erratic patterns as if the mountain itself were warning her of the danger that approached.

She gripped the hilt of her dagger tighter, her senses on high alert. The shadows seemed to lengthen as she walked, creeping across the path toward her like fingers reaching from the void. Her pulse quickened, and she glanced over her shoulder, but there was nothing there.

Not yet.

Elara took a deep breath, steadying herself. She had faced danger before. The trials of Dur'Garran had tested her courage, wisdom, and resolve, and she had emerged stronger for it. But this felt different. This was no mere trial—it was an attack. Morgana knew.

A flicker of movement caught her eye. Elara spun, her heart pounding as she scanned the rocks to her left. The mist shifted, and for a moment, she thought she saw something—a shape, darker than the shadows themselves, moving through the fog. But when she blinked, it was gone.

Her instincts screamed at her to move faster.

She broke into a run, her boots kicking up dust as she raced down the narrow mountain path. The relic throbbed in her satchel, its magic pulsing in time with her racing heart. The path twisted and turned, and Elara moved swiftly, her feet finding purchase on the slick stones even as the mist thickened around her.

Then, out of the corner of her eye, she saw them.

Shadows—no longer just tricks of the light or figments of her imagination. They moved through the mist with a predatory grace, darting from one rock to another, closing in on her from all sides. Their forms were indistinct, shifting and writhing as though they were made of smoke and darkness, but their intent was clear.

They were coming for her.

Elara's breath hitched, her pulse thundering in her ears as she pushed herself harder. The path grew narrower, more treacherous, but there was no turning back. The shadows closed in, their movements fluid and relentless, their whispers filling the air like the rustle of dead leaves.

"You cannot escape," they hissed, their voices blending together in a haunting chorus. "You cannot hide."

Elara's heart raced as she reached the edge of the plateau. She had to think, had to find a way to slow them down. Drawing on the magic Theron had taught her, Elara raised her hand and sent a burst of energy toward the nearest shadow. The magic crackled in the air, sparking like lightning as it struck the creature. For a moment, the shadow recoiled, its form rippling as though it had been wounded.

But it didn't stop.

The shadow surged forward, its tendrils of darkness reaching for Elara, its presence cold and suffocating. Elara slashed at it with her dagger, the blade passing through the shadow's form as though it were cutting through mist. The creature hissed, its body dissolving and reforming in an instant, unaffected by the physical attack.

Panic rose in Elara's chest. The shadows couldn't be killed by normal means—she would have to rely on her magic. But her powers, though growing, were still new and untested. She wasn't sure she could fight off so many at once.

Another shadow lunged at her from the side, and Elara barely had time to react, throwing up a shield of magic just as its tendrils lashed out. The shield held, but the force of the impact sent Elara stumbling backward, her feet slipping on the loose gravel.

She couldn't keep this up. The shadows were everywhere now, surrounding her, their forms flickering and shifting as they moved in for the kill.

Elara's mind raced, searching for a way out. She couldn't fight them all, not like this. She needed to escape, to find cover, to regroup. But the path behind her was blocked, and the shadows were closing in.

Then, from the depths of her memory, she heard Theron's voice.

"Use the terrain," he had said during one of their training sessions. "The land itself can be a weapon if you know how to wield it."

Elara's eyes darted to the rocky cliffs that rose on either side of the path. The stone was jagged and unstable, the perfect target for a well-placed spell.

Without hesitation, Elara summoned her magic, drawing on the energy that pulsed in her chest. She raised her hand, focusing all of her will on the cliffs above her. The air crackled with power, and with a sharp, decisive gesture, she sent a surge of magic toward the rocks.

The ground trembled, and the cliffside groaned in response. A rumble echoed through the air, growing louder and more ominous with each passing second. Elara braced herself as the rocks above began to shift, then tumble, crashing down onto the path below in a cascade of stone and dust.

The shadows shrieked as the rocks fell, their forms scattering as the avalanche swept over them. For a moment, the air was filled with the sound of stone against stone, the ground shaking beneath Elara's feet as the cliffs collapsed.

When the dust finally settled, the shadows were gone.

Elara stood panting, her body trembling from the effort of the spell. The path ahead was blocked by the rubble, but for now, the immediate danger had passed. She had bought herself some time.

But as she took a moment to catch her breath, Elara knew that the shadows were only the beginning. Morgana wouldn't stop until she had destroyed Elara, and the Dark Queen's wrath would not be easily quelled.

Wiping the sweat from her brow, Elara glanced at the relic in her satchel. Its magic hummed softly, but there was a sense of urgency in its pulse, as though it, too, knew that time was running out.

Elara couldn't linger here. She had to move, had to continue her journey. The next relic awaited her, hidden deep within the Emerald Marshes—a place just as dangerous, if not more so, than Dur'Garran.

With a final glance at the collapsed path behind her, Elara turned and made her way down the mountain, her heart heavy with the knowledge that the worst was yet to come.

Far across the kingdom, in the throne room of Eldore, Morgana's eyes flared with fury as the mirror before her shattered into a thousand pieces. The shadows had failed.

The Dark Queen's hands clenched into fists, her nails digging into her palms as rage boiled within her. Elara had escaped—barely—but she had escaped nonetheless. The girl's magic was growing stronger, and Morgana could feel the weight of the relic pressing against the edges of her power.

It was unacceptable.

With a sweep of her hand, Morgana sent the shattered pieces of the mirror flying across the room, the glass shards embedding themselves in the stone walls with a sharp, metallic sound. The throne room darkened, the shadows growing longer as Morgana's anger deepened.

"Elara," she whispered, her voice dripping with venom. "You may have escaped this time, but you will not succeed. I will see you dead before you take what is mine."

Her mind raced, searching for a new plan. The shadows had been her most loyal servants, but even they had not been enough to stop the Cursed Child. No, if she wanted to end Elara's quest once and for all, she would have to take matters into her own hands.

The Dark Queen rose from her throne, her black robes billowing around her as she strode toward the center of the room. With a flick of her wrist, she summoned a pool of dark energy, its surface swirling like liquid night. Within the depths of the energy, a figure began to take shape—a monstrous creature of shadow and fire, its eyes burning with an unholy light.

Morgana smiled, her teeth gleaming in the dim light.

"Go," she commanded the creature, her voice laced with dark magic. "Find her. Destroy her. And bring me her heart."

The creature bowed its head, its massive form dissolving into the shadows before vanishing from sight. Morgana watched it go, her heart filled with cold satisfaction.

Elara had evaded her once, but she would not escape again.

The Dark Queen's wrath was far from spent.

Elara moved swiftly through the dense undergrowth of the forest at the base of Dur'Garran, her body aching from the battle with the shadows, but her resolve stronger than ever. The relic hummed in her satchel, its magic a constant reminder of the path she had chosen.

She had faced Morgana's minions and survived. But the battle had taken its toll. Her arm throbbed where one of the shadows had grazed her, a dark bruise forming beneath her sleeve, and her energy was dangerously low from the effort of using so much magic.

But Elara couldn't stop. She had no time to rest.

The next relic awaited her in the depths of the Emerald Marshes, and the Dark Queen's forces would not relent. Morgana was coming for her, and Elara knew that each step she took brought her closer to the final confrontation.

Despite the pain and exhaustion, a flicker of hope ignited in her heart. She had faced the Dark Queen's wrath and lived to tell the tale. She was stronger than Morgana realized, and with each relic she gathered, her power would grow.

But as Elara pressed on, the weight of the battle still fresh in her mind, she couldn't shake the feeling that something darker was waiting for her in the shadows.

The true fight was yet to come.

Chapter 9: The Siren's Lair

The waves crashed violently against the rocky cliffs as Elara stood at the edge of the shoreline, staring out at the vast, enchanted sea. The water stretched out endlessly before her, a deep and unforgiving blue, broken only by jagged rocks that jutted out like the bones of some ancient, submerged creature. The wind carried with it the taste of salt and the promise of danger, its icy breath biting through her cloak.

This was the Sea of Sorrows, a place whispered about in tavern tales and sailors' superstitions. It was said that beneath its deceptively calm surface lay the Siren's Lair, home to the creatures that had haunted these waters for centuries. They were beings of beauty and death, their songs sweet enough to draw men to their doom but laced with the venom of destruction. No sailor who had heard the song of the sirens had ever returned to tell the tale.

And yet, it was here that Elara's journey had led her. The second relic lay hidden somewhere within the depths of the sea, protected by the very sirens who had claimed the lives of so many. Theron's teachings echoed in her mind as she recalled the dangers of this place, but the relic was her only chance at defeating the Dark Queen. If she failed here, all hope would be lost.

Elara clenched her fists, her determination hardening. She would not fail. She could not.

But as her eyes scanned the turbulent waters, a realization settled over her: she couldn't do this alone. The sea was treacherous, and navigating it would be impossible without someone who knew these waters well. She needed help—someone who had survived the perils of the Sea of Sorrows, someone skilled enough to brave its dangers and mad enough to take the risk.

A voice called from behind her, rough and weathered by years of shouting into the wind.

"You're not thinking of crossing these waters alone, are you, lass?"

Elara turned to find a man standing a few paces away, his silhouette framed by the mist that clung to the rocky shore. He was tall and broad-shouldered, his dark hair tied back in a loose knot, and his face was weathered by the sun and sea. A long coat, once richly embroidered but now tattered at the edges, hung from his shoulders, and a cutlass was strapped to his waist. He had the look of a man who had seen more than his fair share of battles, and yet his eyes—sharp and gleaming—betrayed a sense of cunning and wit.

Elara studied him for a moment, her instincts on edge. The man looked every bit the pirate, and though she had little reason to trust him, there was something about him that told her he wasn't like the others she had encountered on this journey.

"I don't have much choice," she replied, keeping her tone steady. "I have to get across, and I need to find something that's hidden in the sea."

The man's lips curled into a grin, revealing a flash of white teeth beneath his scruffy beard. "The Siren's Lair, I presume?"

Elara's eyes narrowed. "How do you know about the relic?"

The pirate chuckled, stepping closer until he was just a few feet away. "I've been around these parts long enough to know the tales of the Sirens. And I've seen more than a few treasure hunters come and go, seeking whatever riches or artifacts they think might be hidden in those cursed waters." He paused, his grin fading as his expression grew more serious. "None of them have come back."

Elara swallowed hard, her grip tightening on the hilt of her dagger. "I don't have a choice. I need that relic."

The pirate's gaze flickered to the dagger at her side before returning to her face. "Aye, I figured as much. And what's a little danger to someone like you, eh?" He crossed his arms over his chest, tilting his head as he studied her. "But you're not like the other fools who've come this way. You don't look like you're after gold or glory. What's your game, lass?"

Elara hesitated, unsure of how much to reveal. She had learned to be cautious on this journey, especially when dealing with strangers. But something told her that this man—whoever he was—might be her best chance at surviving the Sea of Sorrows.

"I'm trying to stop the Dark Queen," Elara said finally, her voice low but resolute. "There are three relics that hold the key to breaking her curse. I've already found one, but the second is hidden in the Siren's Lair. I need it if I'm going to have any hope of defeating her."

The pirate's eyes widened slightly at the mention of the Dark Queen, but he quickly masked his surprise with a smirk. "Well now, that's quite the tale. And here I thought you were just another adventurer looking to get rich off the bones of old legends."

"I don't have time for games," Elara said, her patience thinning. "Are you going to help me or not?"

The pirate's grin returned, and he extended a hand toward her. "Name's Captain Varian Blackthorn, and if you're looking to cross the Sea of Sorrows, I'm your man."

Elara eyed his outstretched hand warily but took it after a moment's hesitation. His grip was firm and steady, and there was a spark of something—perhaps trust, or at least mutual respect—that passed between them.

"Captain Blackthorn," she repeated, releasing his hand. "I'm Elara."

Varian nodded, stepping back. "Aye, well, Elara, I hope you're ready for what's to come. The Sirens don't take kindly to intruders in their waters, and their song... well, let's just say it's not something you want to hear."

Elara nodded grimly. "I know. But I'm ready."

Varian glanced at her, his expression thoughtful. "We'll see about that," he muttered before turning toward the shoreline. "My ship's docked just around the bend. We'll set sail at first light."

The morning came swiftly, the sky painted in shades of gray as the sun struggled to pierce through the thick clouds. The Sea of Sorrows lay before them, its waters unnaturally still and shimmering with an eerie light. Varian's ship, *The Revenant*, was a sleek, black-hulled vessel that cut through the waves like a knife through silk. Its sails, though tattered at the edges, were strong and taut, and the crew—rough and grizzled men who had clearly seen their fair share of trouble—moved with practiced efficiency as they prepared the ship for departure.

Elara stood at the bow of the ship, her eyes scanning the horizon as they set sail. The wind tugged at her cloak, and the smell of salt and brine filled her lungs. She could feel the tension in the air, the quiet anticipation of what lay ahead. Varian had warned her that once they entered the sirens' waters, the real danger would begin.

Varian approached her, his hands resting on the hilt of his cutlass as he leaned against the railing. "You ready for this, lass?"

Elara nodded, though her heart raced with a mix of fear and determination. "As ready as I'll ever be."

Varian chuckled. "Good. Just remember what I told you—don't listen to their song. Once you hear it, it's already too late."

Elara swallowed hard, her grip tightening on the railing. She had read stories about the sirens, heard the tales of sailors driven mad by their hypnotic voices, but this was no legend. This was real. And the stakes were higher than ever.

As the ship glided deeper into the sea, the air grew thick with an unnatural stillness. The waves that had once lapped gently against the hull now seemed to recede, leaving behind a glassy surface that reflected the storm clouds overhead. The crew moved in silence, their faces grim, and even Varian seemed more subdued as they approached the heart of the Sea of Sorrows.

Elara felt it before she heard it—a subtle shift in the air, a faint tremor that sent a shiver down her spine. Her pulse quickened as the sound reached her ears: a soft, lilting melody that seemed to rise from the depths of the sea itself. It was faint at first, barely audible over the creaking of the ship's timbers, but it grew steadily louder, its haunting beauty impossible to ignore.

The sirens' song.

Elara gritted her teeth, her heart pounding as she tried to block out the sound. But the melody wrapped itself around her, sweet and seductive, pulling at the edges of her mind. It whispered promises of rest, of peace, of an end to the pain and struggle. It told her to let go, to give in, to sink into the warmth of the sea and forget her burdens.

"No," she whispered, clenching her fists so tightly that her knuckles turned white. "I won't listen."

But the song was relentless, its notes weaving through her thoughts like a spider's web, binding her in a cocoon of longing and despair. The sea seemed to shimmer in time with the melody, the water rippling as if it, too, were alive with the power of the sirens' magic.

Elara glanced at Varian, her eyes wide with fear. "It's getting stronger."

Varian's face was set in grim determination, his jaw clenched as he struggled to resist the pull of the song. "Aye, it always does. But we're almost there—just hold on."

The crew wasn't faring as well. Several of the sailors had stopped working, their eyes glazed over as they stared out at the water, their mouths slightly open as if in a trance. One man began to move toward the edge of the ship, his steps slow and deliberate, as though he were being drawn by an invisible force.

"Stop him!" Elara shouted, but Varian was already moving.

The pirate captain grabbed the sailor by the collar, yanking him back just as the man reached the railing. "Not today, lad," Varian muttered, shoving the man toward another crew member. "Tie him down if you have to."

Elara's heart raced as she fought to keep her mind clear. The song was growing louder now, its hypnotic pull almost unbearable. She could feel it in her bones, in her very soul, calling to her, urging her to surrender.

But she couldn't. She wouldn't.

Taking a deep breath, Elara closed her eyes and reached for the magic within her. She could feel it, warm and familiar, pulsing in time with the beat of her heart. With a surge of willpower, she pushed the sirens' song out of her mind, focusing instead on the magic coursing through her veins. The world around her seemed to blur, the song fading into the background as she wrapped herself in a shield of energy.

When she opened her eyes, the song was still there, but it was distant now, its power weakened by the barrier she had created. Elara let out a breath she hadn't realized she was holding, relief flooding through her.

But the danger was far from over.

As the ship moved closer to the heart of the sea, Elara saw them—figures rising from the water, their forms sleek and shimmering in the dim light. The sirens were beautiful, their long, flowing hair cascading down their backs like liquid silver, their eyes glowing with an eerie, otherworldly light. But there was something dangerous in their beauty, something predatory in the way they moved, their voices weaving together in a haunting chorus that made the air itself tremble.

Varian's hand tightened on his cutlass as the sirens circled the ship, their eyes fixed on the crew. "Don't look at them!" he barked, his voice sharp. "Keep your heads down, or you'll be next."

Elara kept her gaze focused on the deck, her heart pounding as the sirens drew closer. She could feel their magic pressing against her shield, testing its strength, but she held firm. She had to.

The relic was close—she could feel its pull, like a beacon calling to her from the depths of the sea. But how was she supposed to reach it with the sirens surrounding them?

Varian seemed to sense her hesitation. "The relic's at the bottom of the sea," he said, his voice low. "That's where they're keeping it. If you want it, you'll have to go in after it."

Elara's stomach dropped. "In the water? With them?"

"Aye," Varian said grimly. "But don't worry—I'll distract them."

Before Elara could protest, Varian unsheathed his cutlass and strode toward the edge of the ship, his eyes blazing with determination. "Oi! Over here, you fish-faced witches!" he shouted, waving his blade in the air. "Come and get me, if you're brave enough!"

The sirens turned toward him, their eyes narrowing as they hissed in unison. With a burst of speed, they lunged at the ship, their hands clawing at the hull as they tried to pull themselves aboard.

"Now, Elara!" Varian shouted. "Go!"

Elara didn't hesitate. With a deep breath, she vaulted over the side of the ship, plunging into the cold, dark waters below.

The sea swallowed her whole.

The water was freezing, its icy grip stealing the breath from Elara's lungs as she kicked her legs, trying to orient herself. The world beneath the surface was dark and foreboding, the shadows of the sea stretching out around her like the arms of some great beast. But the relic was close—she could feel its magic, pulsing faintly through the water.

Elara swam deeper, her heart pounding in her chest as she searched for the source of the magic. The sirens' song was muffled beneath the water, but she could still feel its pull, like a distant echo that tugged at the edges of her mind.

Finally, she saw it—a faint glow, deep beneath the surface. The relic.

It was a small, golden trident, its surface etched with intricate runes that glowed with an otherworldly light. It was embedded in the rocky seafloor, surrounded by a swirling vortex of magic that pulsed in time with the song of the sirens.

Elara swam toward it, her fingers outstretched, but just as she reached for the trident, a figure appeared before her, blocking her path.

A siren.

The creature was even more terrifying up close, its eyes glowing with malice as it hissed at her, its sharp teeth bared in a snarl. Its hands, webbed and clawed, lashed out toward Elara, but she dodged, her magic flaring to life as she pushed the siren back with a burst of energy.

The siren shrieked, its body dissolving into the water, but Elara knew more would come. She didn't have much time.

With a surge of determination, Elara reached for the trident, her fingers closing around its smooth surface. The moment she touched it, a wave of energy surged through her, filling her with a sense of power and purpose.

The relic was hers.

But as Elara turned to swim back to the surface, the water around her seemed to come alive. The sirens were everywhere, their forms swirling through the water like sharks, their eyes locked on her with deadly intent.

Elara's heart raced as she kicked toward the surface, her magic crackling around her as she fought to keep the sirens at bay. But they were relentless, their claws tearing at her as they tried to drag her down into the depths.

Just as Elara thought she wouldn't make it, a hand reached down from above, grabbing her by the arm and hauling her out of the water.

Varian.

The pirate captain grunted as he pulled her onto the deck of the ship, his cutlass flashing as he fended off the remaining sirens. "Got it?" he asked, his voice strained as he fought.

Elara nodded, clutching the trident tightly in her hand. "I've got it."

Varian flashed her a grin. "Then let's get out of here."

The sirens let out one final, furious shriek as Varian steered the ship away from the Sea of Sorrows, their song fading into the distance as the ship sailed into safer waters.

Elara collapsed onto the deck, her body trembling from the effort, but a smile tugged at her lips. She had done it. She had retrieved the second relic.

But as she lay there, catching her breath, Elara knew that the hardest part of her journey was still to come.

The Dark Queen was waiting, and with each relic she gathered, the battle for Eldore drew nearer.

The final confrontation was inevitable, and Elara would need all the strength and courage she had left to face it.

Chapter 10: The Trial of the Moon Temple

The moon hung high in the sky, casting an ethereal glow over the landscape as Elara stood at the base of the Moon Temple. It was a grand structure, carved into the side of a mountain and seemingly untouched by time. The temple had been hidden for centuries, its existence known only to those who still whispered the old stories of the moon goddess, Liriel. The third and final relic—the last key to breaking Morgana's curse—was said to be hidden within these sacred walls. But as Elara stared up at the massive stone pillars that framed the entrance, she knew that retrieving it would not be easy.

The temple was ancient, built long before the kingdoms of Eldore had risen or fallen. It was a place of reverence, dedicated to the worship of the moon and the cycles of life and death that it represented. But it was also a place of trials—trials that would test not only Elara's magic but also her spirit. Theron had warned her that the Moon Temple was unlike any other challenge she had faced. It was not simply a matter of strength or strategy. The temple would force her to confront the darkness within herself, to face the fears and doubts she had long buried.

Elara took a deep breath, her fingers brushing against the relics she had already gathered, now safely tucked into her satchel. Each one pulsed with a quiet, steady power, but they would not help her here. This trial, she would have to face alone.

With a final glance at the moonlit sky, Elara stepped forward and crossed the threshold of the temple.

The air inside the Moon Temple was cool and heavy, thick with the scent of incense and old magic. The walls were lined with intricate carvings of the moon goddess, her figure depicted in various stages of transformation—from a young maiden bathed in the light of a crescent moon, to a wise crone shrouded in shadow. Elara felt a sense of reverence as she walked deeper into the temple, her footsteps echoing softly against the stone floor.

The first chamber she entered was vast, the ceiling rising high above her, its surface painted with scenes of the night sky. In the center of the room stood a large stone altar, upon which lay a single silver chalice, its surface gleaming in the moonlight that streamed in through a narrow window. Elara approached the altar cautiously, her eyes scanning the room for any sign of danger.

As she drew closer, a voice echoed through the chamber—soft, melodic, and filled with an ancient wisdom.

"Welcome, child of the moon."

Elara froze, her heart skipping a beat as the voice seemed to surround her, coming from nowhere and everywhere at once. She turned, her hand instinctively going to the hilt of her dagger, but there was no one there. The chamber was empty, save for the altar and the chalice.

"You have come seeking the final relic," the voice continued, its tone gentle yet filled with a weight of expectation. "But to claim it, you must first prove yourself worthy."

Elara swallowed hard, her pulse quickening. She had expected this. The trials. The tests. But now that she was here, standing in the temple's sacred halls, the reality of what she was about to face felt overwhelming.

"Who are you?" she asked, her voice steady despite the fear that gnawed at her insides.

The air around her shimmered, and for a brief moment, Elara thought she saw a figure—vaguely humanoid, draped in silver light—standing near the altar. But just as quickly as it appeared, the figure vanished, leaving only the voice.

"I am the guardian of the Moon Temple, the keeper of Liriel's sacred relics. I have watched over this place for centuries, waiting for the one who is destined to carry out the goddess's will."

Elara felt a chill run down her spine. "And what must I do to prove myself?"

"The trials you face here will test not only your strength but also your heart," the voice replied. "You must confront the darkness that lies within you, the fears you have long hidden from, and the doubts that cloud your path. Only by emerging from the shadows of your own soul will you be deemed worthy of the relic."

Elara's grip tightened on her dagger, but she nodded. She had faced many dangers on this journey, but nothing as personal as this. And yet, if she had any hope of defeating Morgana and saving Eldore, she knew she had no choice.

"I'm ready," she said, her voice filled with quiet resolve.

The air in the chamber seemed to shift, growing thicker as the walls around her shimmered with magic. The silver chalice on the altar began to glow, its light brightening until it filled the entire room. Elara shielded her eyes from the blinding light, her heart racing as the ground beneath her feet seemed to tremble.

Then, just as suddenly as it had started, the light faded, and Elara found herself standing in a different place entirely.

The first trial began in a forest—one that Elara recognized all too well. The trees were tall and ancient, their gnarled branches reaching toward the sky like skeletal hands. The air was thick with the scent of pine and damp earth, and the only sound was the soft rustle of leaves in the wind. It was the Forbidden Forest, the place where Elara had spent much of her childhood, and where she had first felt the pull of magic.

But something was wrong.

The forest was darker than she remembered, the shadows deeper and more menacing. The trees seemed to loom over her, their branches twisting and writhing as though they were alive. Elara took a step forward, her heart pounding in her chest as she realized what this place truly was.

It was not just the Forbidden Forest. It was a reflection of her own fear.

The ground beneath her feet shifted, and Elara stumbled as the world around her seemed to warp and twist. The trees closed in on her, their branches reaching out like claws, their bark whispering her name.

"Elara... Elara..."

She spun around, her breath coming in ragged gasps as the voices grew louder, more insistent. They were the voices of the villagers from Ashbourne, the people she had grown up with, the people who had always looked at her with suspicion and fear. They had never understood her, never trusted her. They had always whispered behind her back, calling her strange, different, dangerous.

And now, those voices surrounded her, filling the air with accusations and doubts.

"You're nothing but a child playing at being a hero," one voice sneered, its tone dripping with disdain.

"You'll never defeat the Dark Queen," another voice hissed. "You're too weak, too afraid."

Elara's heart raced, her pulse thundering in her ears as the voices pressed in on her, suffocating her with their weight. She could feel the fear rising in her chest, the same fear she had carried with her for years—the fear that she wasn't enough. That she couldn't do this. That she would fail.

The forest seemed to grow darker, the trees closing in on her, their branches wrapping around her like chains. Elara fell to her knees, her hands trembling as she struggled to breathe. The voices were relentless, tearing at her, pulling her down into the darkness.

But then, through the chaos, another voice cut through the noise.

"Elara."

It was soft, barely more than a whisper, but it was enough to pull her from the edge of despair. Elara lifted her head, her breath coming in shallow gasps as she looked around.

The voice came again, stronger this time. "Elara, remember who you are."

Elara's heart skipped a beat. It was her mother's voice.

For a moment, the world seemed to still, and Elara closed her eyes, letting the sound of her mother's voice wash over her. It had been so long since she had heard it, but the memory was still as vivid as ever. Her mother had always been her source of strength, the one who had believed in her even when no one else did.

"Remember what I taught you," her mother's voice whispered. "You are stronger than you know. The darkness cannot claim you unless you let it."

Elara took a deep breath, her mind clearing as the fear that had gripped her began to loosen its hold. The voices of the villagers still echoed around her, but they were quieter now, their power fading as she focused on her mother's words.

"You are not alone," her mother's voice continued. "You have the strength to face this."

Elara opened her eyes, her heart steadying as she rose to her feet. The forest still loomed around her, dark and menacing, but she was no longer afraid. She had faced her fears before, and she would face them again.

"I am stronger than this," Elara whispered, her voice filled with quiet determination.

The shadows that had wrapped around her began to fade, the trees pulling back as the forest lightened. The voices of the villagers grew distant, their accusations losing their power over her.

Elara took a step forward, and the ground beneath her feet steadied. She was no longer lost in the forest of her fears. She had found her way.

The first trial was over.

The second trial began in darkness.

Elara found herself standing in a vast, empty void, the only sound the steady beat of her own heart. There was no light, no sense of direction, only the suffocating weight of the emptiness that surrounded her.

The voice of the guardian echoed through the void, soft and distant.

"Now, you must face the truth of your destiny."

Elara's breath caught in her throat as the words sank in. The truth of her destiny. It was something she had never fully confronted, something she had avoided thinking about for as long as possible.

For years, she had known that she was different. That she was connected to something greater than herself. But the full weight of what that meant had never truly settled on her until now.

"You are the one foretold in the prophecy," the voice continued. "The one destined to break the Dark Queen's curse. But with that destiny comes a choice. You must decide who you will become."

Elara's heart raced as the darkness around her seemed to press in, the weight of the choice bearing down on her. She had never asked for this—never asked to be the one chosen to stop Morgana, to carry the burden of the prophecy. And yet, here she was, standing on the edge of a decision that would determine the fate of the entire kingdom.

"You have the power to break the curse," the voice whispered. "But that power comes at a cost. You must be willing to sacrifice everything to see it through."

Elara swallowed hard, her mind racing. Sacrifice. She had known from the beginning that this journey would require sacrifices—of time, of safety, of certainty. But now, standing in the darkness, the full weight of what that meant became clear.

If she succeeded in breaking the curse, she would have to give up the life she had known. She would never be able to return to the quiet village of Ashbourne, to the simple life she had once dreamed of. She would be a part of something much larger, something far more dangerous. And if she failed... if she failed, the darkness would consume not only her but the entire kingdom.

"You must choose," the voice said softly. "Will you embrace your destiny, or will you turn away from it?"

Elara stood in the darkness, her heart pounding in her chest. The choice felt overwhelming, impossible. But deep down, she knew what she had to do. She had known from the moment she first set out on this journey.

"I choose to fight," Elara said, her voice steady and resolute. "I choose to embrace my destiny."

The darkness around her seemed to lift, a faint light glowing in the distance. The void began to dissolve, and Elara felt the weight of her decision settle over her like a mantle of responsibility. It was heavy, but it was also empowering.

She had made her choice.

The second trial was over.

The final trial was the most difficult of all.

Elara found herself standing in a small room, the walls lined with mirrors. Each one reflected a different version of herself—some older, some younger, some filled with sorrow, others with anger. It was a strange, disorienting place, and Elara's heart raced as she realized what this trial would be.

The voice of the guardian echoed through the room.

"Here, you must confront the many faces of yourself. Only by understanding who you truly are can you claim the relic."

Elara took a deep breath, her eyes scanning the reflections. They were all her, but they were also different—representations of the many paths her life could have taken. The girl she had been before her parents died. The woman she could have become had she stayed in Ashbourne. The warrior she was now, standing at the edge of destiny.

As she looked into each mirror, Elara felt a wave of emotion wash over her—grief, regret, anger, fear. Each reflection was a reminder of the choices she had made, the sacrifices she had endured. But they were also a reminder of her strength, her resilience.

Slowly, Elara approached the largest mirror in the center of the room. Her reflection stared back at her, calm and steady, but there was something different about this version of herself. This was not the Elara she had been, nor the Elara she was now. This was the Elara she would become.

The final trial was not about facing an external enemy or overcoming a magical challenge. It was about accepting herself—her past, her present, and her future.

Elara reached out, her fingers brushing against the cool surface of the mirror. As she did, the reflection began to glow, the light spreading until it filled the entire room.

The voice of the guardian spoke one final time.

"You have faced the trials of the Moon Temple and emerged victorious. You are worthy of the relic."

The light faded, and when Elara opened her eyes, she was standing once again in the main chamber of the temple. The silver chalice on the altar glowed brightly, and beside it lay the third relic—a small, crescent-shaped amulet, its surface etched with the symbols of the moon goddess.

Elara approached the altar, her heart filled with a sense of awe and reverence. She reached out and took the amulet in her hand, feeling its power surge through her.

The third relic was hers.

But as Elara stood in the temple's sacred halls, the weight of her journey still pressing heavily on her, she knew that the hardest part was still to come.

The final confrontation with the Dark Queen was drawing closer, and with each relic she gathered, the battle for the fate of Eldore grew nearer.

Elara had faced the trials of the Moon Temple and emerged stronger, but the real test was still ahead.

And she would be ready.

As Elara left the Moon Temple, the amulet glowing softly in her hand, she felt a deep sense of clarity settle over her. She had been tested in ways she had never imagined, but she had emerged with not only the final relic but also a deeper understanding of herself and her destiny.

The moon hung high in the sky, its light guiding her path as she descended the mountain, her thoughts filled with the challenges that lay ahead. The relics were in her possession, but Morgana's power was growing, and the final battle was inevitable.

Elara's heart raced with anticipation and fear, but she knew one thing for certain:

She was ready to face whatever came next.

Chapter 11: The Betrayal

The sun had barely begun to rise, casting a pale orange glow over the horizon, when Elara returned from the Moon Temple with the third and final relic. It was nestled securely in her satchel, the crescent-shaped amulet glowing faintly against her chest. As she descended the mountains, her thoughts were heavy with the weight of the relic and the trials she had faced to claim it. The Temple had tested not only her strength and magic but also her spirit. She had emerged stronger and more certain of her path, but she knew that the hardest part of her journey still lay ahead.

The Dark Queen, Morgana, was waiting. With each relic Elara had gathered, Morgana's awareness of her quest had grown stronger. The Queen's dark forces were closing in, and the final battle was inevitable. Elara's heart raced at the thought of the confrontation that loomed on the horizon, but she steeled herself. She had come too far to falter now.

By the time Elara reached the village at the foot of the mountain, the sun was high in the sky, casting long shadows over the narrow streets. This was where she had agreed to meet Captain Varian Blackthorn and the crew of *The Revenant*. Varian had proven to be an unlikely but valuable ally in her quest, guiding her through the treacherous waters of the Sea of Sorrows and helping her retrieve the second relic. Now, with the final relic in hand, Elara hoped that his skill and cunning would aid her in the battle against Morgana's forces.

As Elara approached the small inn where they had arranged to meet, her footsteps slowed. Something felt wrong. The village was unusually quiet, its streets eerily empty. There was no sound of the bustling market, no chatter of villagers going about their daily business. A cold sense of unease settled over her, and she instinctively reached for the hilt of her dagger.

The door to the inn was ajar.

Elara's pulse quickened as she pushed the door open, her eyes scanning the room. Inside, the common area was deserted, save for the overturned tables and broken chairs scattered across the floor. The air was thick with the smell of smoke and blood, and Elara's heart dropped into her stomach as she took in the scene of chaos before her.

"Varian?" she called out, her voice barely above a whisper.

There was no answer.

Elara moved deeper into the inn, her hand tightening around her dagger. Her footsteps echoed in the silence, each step feeling heavier than the last. She rounded the corner into the back room, and that's when she saw him.

Varian lay slumped against the far wall, his face pale and his clothes torn and bloodied. His eyes were closed, his chest barely rising and falling with shallow breaths. Elara rushed to his side, dropping to her knees as she reached for his wrist, checking for a pulse.

It was faint, but it was there.

"Varian," she whispered, her voice tight with fear. "What happened?"

His eyelids fluttered, and he groaned softly as his eyes slowly opened. He looked up at her, his expression clouded with pain and regret.

"It was a trap," he muttered, his voice weak but filled with urgency. "They... they knew we were coming."

Elara's heart pounded in her chest. "Who? Who did this?"

Varian coughed, wincing in pain as he struggled to sit up. "Someone... someone tipped them off. The Dark Queen's forces were waiting for us. We didn't stand a chance."

Elara felt a cold knot of dread tighten in her stomach. She had been so careful, so meticulous in planning every step of this journey. How could they have known? How could Morgana's forces have been waiting for them?

"Who betrayed us?" she asked, her voice shaking with anger and fear.

Varian's eyes darkened, and for a moment, he hesitated. "It... it was someone close to you."

Elara's breath caught in her throat, her mind racing as she tried to process his words. Someone close to her? But who? Who could have possibly betrayed her? She had trusted so few people on this journey, had kept her circle small and tight. The thought of betrayal from within sent a wave of nausea crashing over her.

"Who?" she demanded, her voice barely more than a whisper.

Varian closed his eyes, as though the weight of the truth was too much to bear. "Theron."

The world seemed to tilt beneath Elara's feet.

"No," she whispered, shaking her head in disbelief. "No, that's not possible. Theron wouldn't—"

But even as the words left her lips, doubt began to creep into her mind. Theron had been her mentor, the one who had taught her how to harness her magic, how to navigate the dangers of the dark forces that surrounded her. He had guided her, supported her, been a crucial ally in her fight against Morgana. But there had always been something... distant about him. Something he had never fully revealed.

Varian's hand tightened weakly around her wrist. "I didn't want to believe it either," he said, his voice strained. "But it's true. He's been working with the Dark Queen all along."

Elara felt as though the ground had been ripped out from beneath her. Betrayal. From the one person she had trusted most. The one person who had been there from the beginning. It didn't make sense. How could Theron, who had taught her so much, who had guided her through the trials of magic, have been a traitor?

"Why?" she asked, her voice shaking. "Why would he do this?"

Varian's gaze softened with sympathy. "I don't know his reasons, lass. But the fact remains—he's been playing both sides. And now, Morgana's forces are closing in. We have to get out of here."

Elara's mind raced, her thoughts a whirlwind of confusion and pain. Theron's betrayal cut deeper than any physical wound, shaking the foundation of everything she had believed. How long had he been working with Morgana? Had he ever truly been on her side, or had he been manipulating her from the very beginning?

The anger bubbled up inside her, hot and fierce. She had been used, played like a pawn in a game she hadn't even known she was a part of. But now, she was faced with a choice. She could let this betrayal break her, or she could rise above it.

Elara took a deep breath, steadying herself. She couldn't afford to let this defeat her. The final battle was still ahead, and Morgana was still the true enemy.

Whatever Theron's reasons, whatever his betrayal, Elara would face it. But not now. Not while the Dark Queen's forces were closing in.

"We need to move," Elara said, her voice hardening with resolve. "Can you walk?"

Varian grimaced but nodded. "I've had worse."

With her help, Varian struggled to his feet, his face pale but determined. Elara glanced around the wrecked inn, her mind racing as she tried to formulate a plan. The Dark Queen's forces were likely already on their way, and they couldn't stay here much longer. They needed to regroup, to find safety, and prepare for what was to come.

But as they made their way to the door, Elara's heart was heavy with the weight of the betrayal. Theron had been more than just a mentor to her—he had been a guide, a figure she had looked up to in the darkest moments of her journey. To learn that he had been working against her all along... it was almost too much to bear.

But there was no time to dwell on it now. Elara would confront him, she would demand answers—but first, she had to survive.

The forest was thick with shadows as Elara and Varian made their way through the underbrush, moving quickly but cautiously. Varian had recovered enough to walk on his own, though his movements were slow and labored, his injuries clearly taking their toll. Still, he pressed on, his expression grim and focused.

Elara's mind was a whirlwind of emotions as they traveled. Betrayal, anger, confusion—they all swirled together, making it hard to focus. But beneath it all was a sense of urgency. Morgana's forces were closing in, and they had to stay ahead of them.

"We need to get to the others," Varian said, his voice low. "The crew will be waiting for us at the safehouse. We can regroup there."

Elara nodded, though her thoughts were elsewhere. "What about Theron? What do we do about him?"

Varian's eyes darkened. "We deal with him when the time comes. Right now, we need to focus on staying alive."

Elara couldn't argue with that. But the thought of confronting Theron filled her with a mixture of dread and anger. She needed to understand why he had betrayed her. What had driven him to side with Morgana after everything they had been through?

As they continued through the forest, the sound of movement in the trees ahead made them both stop in their tracks. Elara's hand went to her dagger, and Varian unsheathed his cutlass, his body tensing as they waited for the source of the noise to reveal itself.

A figure stepped out from the shadows.

It was one of Varian's crew members, a wiry man with a scar running down the side of his face. He looked winded, his clothes torn and his face pale.

"Captain," he gasped, doubling over as he caught his breath. "We've been compromised. The Dark Queen's forces are already at the safehouse."

Varian cursed under his breath. "How far ahead are they?"

"Not far," the man replied, his voice tight with urgency. "We've been trying to hold them off, but we can't keep it up much longer. They'll be here any minute."

Elara's heart raced. They were out of time.

"We have to move," she said, turning to Varian. "Now."

Varian nodded, his expression grim. "Aye. Let's go."

They moved quickly, cutting through the trees as they made their way toward the safehouse. Elara's mind raced, her thoughts filled with the impending confrontation. She had faced many dangers on this journey, but none as personal as this. The betrayal from someone she had trusted so deeply weighed heavily on her, but she couldn't let it shake her resolve.

As they approached the clearing where the safehouse was hidden, the sound of clashing steel and shouted orders reached their ears. Elara's heart pounded in her chest as they neared the battle, her grip tightening on her dagger.

The safehouse was surrounded.

Morgana's forces had already breached the perimeter, their dark-clad soldiers moving through the trees like shadows. The few remaining members of Varian's crew were locked in battle, their swords flashing in the dim light as they fought to hold their ground.

Elara's eyes scanned the battlefield, her heart racing. She couldn't see Theron among the combatants, but she knew he had to be close. He wouldn't betray her and then simply disappear. No—he would be here, watching, waiting.

Elara drew her dagger, her magic crackling at the edges of her consciousness as she prepared to fight. But before she could move, a voice called out from the edge of the clearing.

"Elara."

She froze, her blood turning to ice in her veins.

Theron stepped out from the shadows, his face unreadable as he approached her. His long, dark cloak billowed in the wind, and his eyes gleamed with a cold, calculating light.

Elara's heart pounded in her chest as she stared at him, her mind racing. This was the man who had guided her, taught her, been a mentor to her in her darkest moments. And now, he stood before her as her betrayer.

"Why?" she asked, her voice shaking with anger and hurt. "Why did you betray me?"

Theron's expression softened, but there was no regret in his eyes. "I did what I had to do, Elara. You were never meant to win this fight."

Elara's blood boiled at his words. "You've been working with Morgana all along?"

Theron's lips curled into a bitter smile. "Not always. But Morgana's power is greater than you can imagine. The curse that binds her to the throne is not something you can simply break with relics and spells. It's far more complex than that. And the cost of breaking it... is more than you can bear."

Elara shook her head, her heart breaking at the realization that everything she had believed, everything Theron had taught her, had been a lie. "You lied to me. You used me."

"I guided you," Theron said, his voice calm, almost patronizing. "I helped you become strong enough to face her. But now, you must understand—this fight cannot be won."

Elara's anger flared, her magic surging to the surface as she stepped toward him. "I won't stop fighting, Theron. I don't care what you say. I will defeat her."

Theron's eyes darkened, and for the first time, a flicker of sadness crossed his face. "Then you will die trying."

The ground beneath them trembled, and Elara felt the weight of the dark magic in the air as Morgana's forces closed in. The final battle had begun.

But despite the betrayal, despite the heartbreak, Elara's resolve was stronger than ever.

With the support of her allies, she would face whatever came next. And she would not fail.

Chapter 12: The Siege of the Dark Castle

The Dark Castle loomed before them, its towering spires cutting through the sky like jagged claws. Dark clouds swirled around the fortress, casting an eerie shadow over the land, and the air was thick with the stench of old magic. Elara stood at the edge of the forest, her heart pounding as she gazed up at the place where her final confrontation with Morgana, the Dark Queen, would take place. The fortress was a place of twisted beauty, its walls adorned with intricate carvings and ancient symbols, but beneath the surface, it pulsed with a malevolent energy that set Elara's nerves on edge.

Beside her, Captain Varian Blackthorn surveyed the castle with narrowed eyes, his hand resting on the hilt of his cutlass. His crew, battle-hardened and grim-faced, stood behind him, their weapons at the ready. Elara's other companions, a motley group of fighters and mages who had joined her along the way, formed a loose circle around her, their expressions a mix of fear and determination.

Elara's fingers brushed against the relics in her satchel, their magic thrumming with a quiet, steady pulse. The three relics—the orb, the trident, and the crescent-shaped amulet—were the key to breaking the curse that bound Morgana to her throne. But as powerful as the relics were, Elara couldn't shake the feeling that they might not be enough. Morgana's power was ancient and deeply rooted in dark magic. The Dark Queen had ruled over Eldore for decades, her influence spreading like a poison across the kingdom. And now, Elara and her companions were preparing to storm the heart of that darkness.

"We don't have much time," Varian said, breaking the tense silence. "Morgana knows we're coming. If we don't move now, her forces will overwhelm us before we even reach the gates."

Elara nodded, her pulse quickening as she turned to face her companions. "This is it," she said, her voice steady but laced with the weight of what was to come. "Once we enter the castle, there's no turning back. Morgana will throw everything she has at us. But we have to keep moving forward. The relics are the only way to break the curse, and we can't let her stop us."

Varian's crew murmured their agreement, their faces hardening with resolve. The tension in the air was palpable, the weight of the upcoming battle pressing down on them all. Elara could feel her own fear gnawing at the edges of her mind, but she pushed it aside. She couldn't afford to hesitate now. Too much was at stake.

Taking a deep breath, Elara stepped forward, her eyes locked on the towering gates of the Dark Castle. The final battle had begun.

The moment they crossed the threshold into the castle grounds, the air grew colder, and Elara could feel the dark magic that infused every stone of the fortress. The gates creaked open with an ominous groan, revealing a long, winding path that led up to the main entrance. The walls on either side were lined with grotesque statues of twisted creatures, their eyes gleaming in the dim light as if they were watching the intruders' every move.

As Elara and her companions made their way toward the castle, the ground beneath their feet trembled, and the statues began to stir. Their stone forms cracked and shifted, and with a series of loud, grinding noises, the creatures came to life. They stepped down from their pedestals, their jagged claws scraping against the cobblestones as they moved toward the group with a predatory grace.

"Traps," Varian muttered, his hand tightening on his cutlass. "Of course."

The first of the creatures lunged at them, its massive jaws snapping inches from Elara's face. She ducked just in time, her dagger flashing as she slashed at the creature's side. The blade glanced off its stone hide, barely leaving a mark. Another creature attacked from behind, its claws raking the air as Varian parried the blow with his sword, driving it back with a powerful strike.

"These things are tough," Varian growled, his face twisted in concentration as he fought off another attacker. "We can't just brute force our way through them."

Elara's mind raced as she tried to think of a solution. The creatures were clearly animated by Morgana's magic, their stone forms impervious to normal weapons. They needed something more powerful to break through.

"The relics," she said suddenly, her hand going to the satchel at her side. "We can use the relics."

Varian glanced at her, his eyes flashing with uncertainty. "Are you sure? We might need their power for later."

"We don't have a choice," Elara said, her voice firm. "If we don't stop these things now, we'll never make it to the throne room."

Without waiting for a response, Elara reached into the satchel and pulled out the orb, its surface pulsing with a faint blue light. She closed her eyes, focusing on the magic within the relic, and felt the power surge through her. The air around her crackled with energy as she raised the orb, its light growing brighter with each passing second.

With a shout, Elara released the magic, sending a wave of energy crashing into the stone creatures. The force of the blast shattered their stone forms, sending shards of rock flying in all directions. The creatures crumbled to the ground, their magic dissipating into the air like smoke.

The path ahead was clear.

Elara let out a breath she hadn't realized she was holding, her body trembling from the exertion of the spell. The orb's light dimmed, its power temporarily spent, but it had done its job. They could move forward.

"Let's keep moving," Elara said, her voice tight with urgency. "We're running out of time."

THE INTERIOR OF THE Dark Castle was even more foreboding than the outside. The walls were made of dark stone, lit only by the faint glow of torches mounted at intervals along the hallway. The air was thick with the scent of old magic and decay, and every step they took echoed eerily through the corridors.

As they moved deeper into the castle, the sense of danger grew. Elara could feel Morgana's presence, her dark magic pressing in on them from all sides. The Queen was waiting for them, her power thrumming through the very walls of the fortress.

They encountered more traps as they made their way through the castle—hidden pits that opened beneath their feet, walls that closed in on them with crushing force, and magical wards that sent searing blasts of energy at anyone who got too close. But with each challenge, Elara and her companions pressed on, their determination unshaken.

As they approached the final set of doors that led to the throne room, the atmosphere shifted. The air grew colder, and the shadows in the corners of the room seemed to stretch and writhe as though they were alive. Elara's heart pounded in her chest as she reached for the door, her hand trembling with both fear and anticipation.

This was it.

Beyond this door was Morgana, the Dark Queen who had ruled over Eldore with an iron fist for decades. Elara had spent her entire journey preparing for this moment, gathering the relics and building her strength. But now, standing at the threshold of the final battle, doubt began to creep into her mind.

Was she truly ready? Could she really defeat Morgana, whose power was unlike anything Elara had ever faced?

A hand on her shoulder pulled her from her thoughts. Elara turned to see Varian standing beside her, his expression grim but determined.

"You've got this, lass," he said, his voice low and steady. "We're with you."

Elara nodded, drawing strength from his words. She couldn't let fear control her. She had come too far, fought too hard, to back down now.

Taking a deep breath, she pushed open the doors.

The throne room was vast, its ceiling soaring high above them and supported by massive stone pillars that glowed faintly with an unnatural light. At the far end of the room, on a raised platform, sat Morgana, the Dark Queen. She was draped in black robes that shimmered like liquid night, her long, dark hair cascading down her shoulders. Her eyes, glowing with an eerie light, were fixed on Elara, and a cold smile played at her lips.

"Welcome, Elara," Morgana said, her voice smooth and filled with dark amusement. "I've been expecting you."

Elara's heart pounded in her chest as she stepped forward, her hand tightening around the hilt of her dagger. Behind her, Varian and the others spread out, their weapons at the ready.

"You know why I'm here," Elara said, her voice steady despite the fear that gripped her. "This ends now, Morgana. Your reign of darkness is over."

Morgana laughed softly, the sound sending a chill down Elara's spine. "Is that what you think?" she asked, rising from her throne. "Do you really believe that a few relics and a ragtag group of rebels can stop me?"

Her eyes flashed with power, and the air around her crackled with dark magic. "You are a fool, Elara. You have no idea what you're up against."

Elara swallowed hard, but she stood her ground. "I know enough. And I have the relics."

Morgana's smile faded, and her eyes darkened. "The relics," she said, her voice laced with disdain. "You think they will save you

? You think they will undo the power that I have spent centuries building?"

She raised her hand, and the room trembled as dark energy swirled around her. "You are nothing, Elara. You are a child playing at being a hero. And now, you will pay the price for your arrogance."

With a wave of her hand, Morgana unleashed a torrent of dark magic, the force of it slamming into Elara like a physical blow. Elara was thrown back, her body crashing into one of the pillars as the breath was knocked from her lungs. Pain lanced through her chest, and for a moment, she couldn't move.

"Elara!" Varian shouted, rushing to her side.

Elara gasped for air, her vision swimming as she tried to pull herself to her feet. Morgana's power was overwhelming, far stronger than anything she had ever faced before. The relics pulsed faintly in her satchel, but their magic felt distant, out of reach.

"Elara," Varian said urgently, pulling her to her feet. "We need to use the relics—now."

Elara nodded, her mind racing as she struggled to focus. The relics were their only chance, but Morgana's power was suffocating, making it difficult to even think.

Gathering what strength she had left, Elara reached into her satchel and pulled out the relics. The orb, the trident, and the amulet glowed faintly in her hands, their power humming softly. But it wasn't enough. They needed more.

"We have to combine their magic," Elara said, her voice tight with pain. "It's the only way."

Varian's eyes widened. "How?"

Elara closed her eyes, focusing on the relics in her hands. She could feel their magic, but it was fragmented, incomplete. She needed to bind them together, to create a single, unified force.

Drawing on the magic that Theron had taught her, Elara began to weave the power of the relics together. The air around her shimmered with energy as the relics pulsed in time with her heartbeat, their light growing brighter with each passing second.

But Morgana was not idle.

With a snarl, the Dark Queen unleashed another wave of magic, the force of it crashing into Elara like a tidal wave. Elara cried out in pain, her knees buckling as the weight of Morgana's power pressed down on her. The relics flickered in her hands, their light dimming as the dark magic threatened to snuff them out.

"Elara!" Varian shouted, his voice filled with desperation.

Elara gritted her teeth, her body trembling from the effort. She couldn't let Morgana win. She couldn't let the darkness consume her.

With a final surge of willpower, Elara unleashed the combined magic of the relics. The room exploded with light as the relics' power surged through the air, their energy crashing into Morgana with a blinding force.

The Dark Queen screamed, her body writhing as the magic tore through her. For a moment, it seemed as though Elara had won, as though the relics' power was enough to break Morgana's hold on the kingdom.

But then, the light faltered.

Morgana's laughter echoed through the throne room, dark and cruel. "Did you really think it would be that easy?" she hissed, her eyes blazing with fury. "You are nothing, Elara. You cannot defeat me."

The darkness surged back, more powerful than before, and Elara felt the relics slip from her grasp as the magic overwhelmed her.

The final battle had only just begun.

Elara's vision blurred as the weight of the dark magic pressed down on her. She could feel the relics slipping through her fingers, their power fading as Morgana's darkness engulfed them. For a moment, it seemed as though all hope was lost—that Morgana's reign of terror would continue, unchallenged, and that Elara had failed.

But then, through the haze of pain and fear, Elara heard a voice.

"You are stronger than this."

It was faint, barely more than a whisper, but it cut through the darkness like a knife. Elara's heart skipped a beat as she recognized the voice.

Her mother's voice.

"You have the strength to face this," the voice whispered. "Do not let the darkness consume you."

Elara's eyes fluttered open, her breath coming in shallow gasps as she stared up at the Dark Queen. Morgana stood before her, her body surrounded by a swirling vortex of dark magic, her eyes blazing with triumph.

But Elara was not finished yet.

With a final surge of strength, Elara reached deep within herself, drawing on the power that had been given to her by the trials, by the relics, and by the strength of her own spirit.

And with a scream, she unleashed it all.

The room erupted with light, brighter and more powerful than anything Elara had ever felt before. The relics, now bound together by Elara's will, surged with energy, their combined magic tearing through Morgana's defenses.

The Dark Queen's scream echoed through the throne room as the magic enveloped her, her body writhing in agony as the relics' power consumed her.

And then, with a final burst of light, Morgana was gone.

The darkness that had filled the room dissipated, leaving behind only silence.

Elara collapsed to the ground, her body trembling with exhaustion as the weight of the battle finally caught up with her.

It was over.

The Dark Queen was defeated.

But as Elara lay on the cold stone floor, her heart still racing from the battle, she knew that the cost of victory had been great.

And the kingdom of Eldore would never be the same.

Chapter 13: The Final Confrontation

The throne room was eerily silent after the whirlwind of the battle. The relics had done their part, and Morgana's forces had retreated, but the air still crackled with tension. The Dark Queen had yet to fall. Elara stood alone in the grand, cavernous hall, her breathing heavy, her body aching from the intense surge of magic she had summoned. Every part of her wanted to believe the worst was over, but she knew better. This was just the beginning of the final test. The battle was far from over.

At the far end of the room, shrouded in shadow, Morgana sat on her throne. The Queen's presence radiated a dark energy that filled the chamber, oppressive and suffocating. Her dark robes shimmered with an unnatural light, and her once-beautiful face was twisted with anger and despair. Yet, there was something almost haunting about her expression—an underlying pain that Elara had never seen before.

The relics had wounded Morgana, but they hadn't broken her.

Elara's heart pounded in her chest as she gathered her strength, knowing that what came next would decide the fate of the entire kingdom. Her hands trembled slightly as she tightened her grip on her dagger, though she knew that this final confrontation would not be won with weapons. It would be won—or lost—by magic.

"I underestimated you," Morgana said, her voice soft but filled with venom. She rose from her throne, her eyes glowing with dark energy as she stepped forward. "I didn't think you would make it this far. But no matter... it will end here."

Elara's heart raced as she took a step back, her eyes never leaving the Queen. She could feel the power radiating from Morgana, stronger and more dangerous than ever. The relics had given Elara a chance, but Morgana's magic was ancient, forged in the darkest corners of the world. She wasn't sure if she had the strength to defeat her.

But she had to try.

"Morgana," Elara called out, her voice steady despite the fear that gripped her. "This doesn't have to end in bloodshed. I have the relics. I can break the curse."

The Queen's lips curled into a cruel smile. "Break the curse?" she repeated, her voice mocking. "Do you really think it's that simple, girl? You think you understand the power of these relics, but you have no idea what they truly are. You are a child playing with forces beyond your comprehension."

Elara's pulse quickened, but she refused to back down. "I understand enough. I know that the curse has bound you to the throne for centuries, but it doesn't have to be this way. You don't have to keep fighting. Let me end this."

Morgana's eyes darkened, and for a moment, something flickered across her face—something that looked almost like regret.

"You think you can save me?" Morgana said, her voice low and dangerous. "You think you can fix what has already been broken? You are more foolish than I thought."

With a wave of her hand, the room erupted in a torrent of dark energy, the air crackling with magic as shadows swirled around them. Elara staggered back, raising her hand to summon a protective barrier, but the force of Morgana's power was overwhelming. The darkness pressed in on her from all sides, threatening to crush her under its weight.

"You don't understand the curse, Elara," Morgana continued, her voice echoing through the chamber. "You never could. The curse is not just a chain that binds me to the throne. It is a part of me. It is my very soul."

Elara gritted her teeth as she struggled to maintain her shield, her body trembling from the effort. "Then tell me," she said, her voice strained. "Tell me the truth."

For a moment, the darkness seemed to hesitate, and Morgana's expression shifted. The mocking cruelty in her eyes faded, replaced by something else—something deeper, more painful. She lowered her hand, and the torrent of magic eased, leaving only a faint shimmer in the air.

"You want to know the truth?" Morgana asked, her voice soft but filled with bitterness. "Fine. I will show you."

The air around them shimmered, and suddenly, the throne room began to dissolve, replaced by a new scene. Elara blinked in surprise as the room melted away, the stone walls giving way to a beautiful garden bathed in moonlight. The air was warm and fragrant, filled with the scent of blooming flowers, and the sound of gentle laughter echoed in the distance.

Elara looked around, confused. "What is this?"

"This," Morgana said, her voice distant, "is where it began."

As Elara turned, she saw a younger version of Morgana standing in the center of the garden. Her dark hair flowed freely down her back, and her face was unlined by the bitterness and cruelty that now marked her features. She was laughing, her eyes bright with joy, and beside her stood a man—a tall, handsome man with kind eyes and a gentle smile. He reached out to take her hand, and Morgana's laughter grew softer, more intimate.

Elara's heart clenched as she watched the scene unfold. This was Morgana, long before she had become the Dark Queen. Long before the curse.

"I was once like you, Elara," Morgana said softly, her voice filled with a sadness that cut through the bitterness. "I was young, full of hope and love. I ruled the kingdom with fairness and kindness, and I thought I would live happily ever after."

The scene shifted, and Elara watched as the younger Morgana walked hand in hand with the man through the garden. But there was a tension in the air now, something darker that began to creep in at the edges of the scene. The moon overhead seemed to dim, and the shadows in the garden lengthened.

"But life is not a fairy tale," Morgana continued, her voice hardening. "The man I loved—he was taken from me. Killed by those who sought power, who envied the peace we had built."

The scene darkened, and Elara watched as the younger Morgana fell to her knees, her face twisted with grief and rage. The garden around her withered, the flowers dying, the trees blackening with rot. The man who had stood beside her was gone, and in his place, there was only emptiness.

"I swore that I would never be powerless again," Morgana said, her voice filled with cold determination. "I sought out the forbidden magic, the dark arts that had been hidden away for centuries. And I found it. I made a pact with forces far older and more powerful than I could have imagined."

The air around them crackled with dark energy, and Elara watched as the younger Morgana rose to her feet, her eyes blazing with fury and desperation. Her hands were outstretched, and dark tendrils of magic wrapped around her, binding her to the throne. The throne room reappeared around them, but this time, it was twisted and warped, filled with shadows and dark power.

"The curse," Morgana said bitterly, "was not something done to me. It was something I chose. I bound myself to this throne, to this kingdom, so that no one could ever take it from me again. But in doing so, I became a prisoner of my own power."

Elara's heart pounded in her chest as the weight of Morgana's words sank in. The curse wasn't just a spell that bound Morgana to the throne—it was something she had willingly accepted. She had chosen the darkness, had embraced the power that now consumed her.

"But why?" Elara asked, her voice filled with a mixture of anger and sorrow. "Why would you do this? You could have chosen another path. You could have—"

"Could have what?" Morgana snapped, her eyes flashing with anger. "Chosen to be weak? To watch as everything I loved was taken from me? You don't understand, Elara. You could never understand."

Elara's heart ached as she stared at the Queen, seeing for the first time the depth of her pain. Morgana wasn't just a villain, a power-hungry ruler who had lost her way. She was a woman who had been broken by grief, who had made a terrible choice in a moment of desperation. And now, she was trapped, unable to escape the darkness she had embraced.

"You're wrong," Elara said quietly, her voice filled with empathy. "I do understand. I've lost people I cared about too. But you didn't have to let it turn you into this."

Morgana's expression hardened, and the darkness in the room thickened. "Enough of this," she hissed, her voice filled with fury. "You think you can judge me? You think you can break this curse?"

The air crackled with power as Morgana raised her hands, dark energy swirling around her like a storm. Elara felt the weight of the magic pressing down on her, suffocating and cold. The final battle was at hand, and Morgana's fury was unrelenting.

"You will fall, Elara," Morgana said, her voice cold and merciless. "Just as everyone before you has fallen."

Elara gritted her teeth, her heart pounding in her chest. She could feel the relics pulsing in her satchel, their power still waiting to be unleashed. But something held her back. Morgana's words, her tragic past, had shaken her resolve.

Could she really defeat Morgana? Could she break the curse without losing herself in the process?

AS THE DARK ENERGY swirled around her, Elara felt a strange, seductive pull at the edges of her mind. It was the same feeling she had sensed during her journey—the temptation of power. The darkness called to her, offering strength, control, and the ability to bend the world to her will. It whispered promises of victory, of immortality, of the power to reshape the kingdom in her image.

All she had to do was take it.

For a moment, Elara hesitated. The darkness was so tempting, so easy. She could feel it in her veins, offering her the power to end the battle, to defeat Morgana once and for all.

But then, she remembered the trials she had faced—the challenges that had tested her courage, her wisdom, and her resolve. She remembered the people who had stood by her, who had believed in her, who had fought alongside her. And she remembered the lessons she had learned—that true strength didn't come from power, but from the choices she made.

Elara took a deep breath, closing her eyes as she centered herself. The darkness was not her path. She had come too far to fall now.

"I won't become like you, Morgana," Elara said, her voice steady and filled with conviction. "I won't let the darkness consume me."

Morgana's eyes flashed with anger, and the storm of magic around her intensified. "Fool!" she spat. "You think you can defeat me with your pathetic ideals? You will fall, just like everyone else."

Elara raised her hand, summoning the magic of the relics. The air around her shimmered with light as the orb, the trident, and the amulet began to glow, their power resonating with her own. She could feel the magic pulsing through her, strong and pure, untainted by darkness.

With a shout, Elara unleashed the full force of the relics, sending a wave of magic crashing toward Morgana. The Queen snarled, raising her own hands to counter the attack, but the power of the relics was too strong. The light of the relics cut through the darkness, their energy tearing through the Queen's defenses.

Morgana screamed as the magic engulfed her, her body writhing in agony as the curse began to unravel. The dark energy that had bound her to the throne for centuries was breaking, dissolving into the air like smoke.

Elara stepped forward, her heart heavy with both triumph and sorrow. Morgana's face twisted in pain, but there was something else in her eyes—something almost like relief.

"You... you don't understand..." Morgana gasped, her voice weak and broken. "The curse... it's... more than just me..."

Elara's heart clenched as she knelt beside the Queen, her hand trembling as she reached out to touch Morgana's shoulder. "What do you mean?"

Morgana's eyes fluttered, her strength fading. "The kingdom... it's bound to the curse. If you break it... everything will fall apart..."

Elara's breath caught in her throat as the full weight of Morgana's words sank in. The curse wasn't just binding Morgana—it was holding the entire kingdom together. If Elara broke it, she wouldn't just destroy the Queen—she would destroy the kingdom itself.

Tears filled Elara's eyes as she stared down at Morgana, the woman who had once been a kind and just ruler, now broken by her own choices. She had fought so hard to defeat the Queen, but now she faced an impossible choice.

Break the curse and risk the collapse of the kingdom, or let Morgana live and allow the darkness to continue.

Elara's hand trembled as she weighed the decision. The fate of Eldore rested in her hands.

But as she looked into Morgana's eyes, she knew what she had to do.

With a heavy heart, Elara summoned the last of her magic and whispered a single word.

"Release."

The light of the relics flared one final time, and with a soft sigh, Morgana's body dissolved into mist, her spirit finally free from the curse that had bound her for so long.

The throne room was silent.

Elara sank to the floor, her body trembling with exhaustion as the weight of her choice settled over her.

The Dark Queen was gone.

But the kingdom's future was uncertain.

And the battle, though won, had come at a terrible cost.

Chapter 14: The Breaking of the Curse

The air was thick with tension, the kind that presses down on your chest and steals the breath from your lungs. Elara stood alone in the vast throne room, her heart pounding as the final echoes of the battle faded into silence. The relics, now glowing faintly, pulsed softly at her side, as though they, too, were waiting for the next move. But for the first time since she had begun her journey, Elara wasn't sure what to do.

Morgana—the Dark Queen—was gone. Her body had dissolved into the mist, her spirit freed from the curse that had bound her to the throne for centuries. But in her final moments, Morgana had revealed a truth that Elara had never anticipated: the curse that held the Dark Queen's power wasn't just a chain around one woman's soul—it was the very force holding the kingdom together. If Elara broke the curse, she risked destroying everything.

The throne room was cold and empty, its stone walls etched with the dark magic that had kept Morgana in power for so long. Shadows flickered across the floor, cast by the pale light of the relics, and Elara felt the weight of her decision pressing down on her with suffocating force.

She had come this far—fought her way through trials and battles, made allies and lost friends, all to end the reign of the Dark Queen. But now, at the precipice of victory, she faced an impossible choice.

"I never wanted this," Elara whispered to the relics, her voice trembling with the weight of what she was about to do. "I never wanted to be the one to decide the fate of the kingdom."

But no matter how much she wished for someone else to bear the burden, it had fallen to her.

The relics, which had guided her through every step of her journey, now pulsed with a gentle warmth, as if urging her forward. They had given her the power to defeat Morgana, but now they asked for something more—something deeper. They asked for a choice.

Elara closed her eyes, her mind racing as she tried to grasp the enormity of the situation. If she chose to break the curse, she would free the kingdom from Morgana's dark magic. The reign of terror would finally end, and the people would be able to rebuild their lives. But it wouldn't be without cost. The curse was woven into the very fabric of the land, and tearing it apart could cause devastation unlike anything the kingdom had seen before.

The throne room flickered with magic, and Elara felt the relics tremble in her hands. She could feel the power within them, waiting for her to make a decision. They were ancient, older than the kingdom itself, and they carried the weight of history with them. But the choice—this final choice—was hers.

Taking a deep breath, Elara stepped forward. The relics flared in response, their light growing brighter as she approached the center of the throne room. She had faced so many trials, so much pain, but this was the final test. This was the moment where everything would be decided.

She reached the base of the throne—the seat of Morgana's power—and knelt before it. The relics pulsed with a steady rhythm, the magic within them humming softly as Elara laid them in front of her. The orb, the trident, and the amulet glowed faintly, their energies swirling together in a dance of light and shadow.

Elara's fingers trembled as she touched the relics, her heart racing with both fear and anticipation. She had faced dark magic before, had even been tempted by it. But this was different. The curse that held the kingdom in its grip wasn't just evil—it was ancient, powerful, and deeply rooted in the land itself. Shattering it would be like tearing a piece of the world apart.

But Elara knew what she had to do.

"I choose the light," she whispered, her voice barely audible in the vast emptiness of the throne room.

With those words, she called upon the magic of the relics, summoning their power with every ounce of strength she had left. The air around her crackled with energy, and the room trembled as the relics began to respond. The orb glowed bright blue, the trident shimmered with silver light, and the amulet pulsed with a soft, golden hue. Together, their magic merged into a single, brilliant force, swirling through the air like a storm of light.

The power was overwhelming, and for a moment, Elara thought she might not be able to control it. The relics surged with ancient energy, their combined strength almost too much for her to bear. But she held on, her heart pounding as she guided the magic toward its final purpose: breaking the curse that had held the kingdom captive for so long.

As the magic swirled around her, the shadows in the throne room began to lift. The dark energy that had suffused the castle for centuries trembled, quivering at the edges as the relics' light began to overpower it. The very walls of the castle seemed to groan in protest, as if the structure itself was trying to hold on to the curse that bound it.

Elara gritted her teeth, her body trembling from the effort. The magic was pushing back against her, resisting her attempts to unravel it. But she refused to give up. She had come too far to fail now.

With a final, desperate surge of willpower, Elara unleashed the full force of the relics, sending a wave of light crashing through the throne room. The dark magic shattered, its hold on the kingdom finally breaking as the curse was torn apart.

The air exploded with energy, and Elara was thrown backward, her body slamming against the cold stone floor. Pain lanced through her chest, and for a moment, she couldn't move. Her vision blurred, and the sound of the relics' magic echoed in her ears, a distant hum that slowly began to fade.

When the light finally dimmed, the throne room was quiet.

Elara lay on the floor, her body trembling with exhaustion as the weight of the battle finally caught up to her. She had done it. The curse was broken.

But as she struggled to sit up, she felt a strange emptiness settle over her. The relics, which had been her companions throughout this entire journey, lay scattered on the floor around her, their light completely extinguished. The magic that had once pulsed through them was gone, and the ancient power they had held was no more.

Elara's heart clenched with a deep sense of loss. The relics had been more than just tools—they had been a part of her, a source of strength and guidance. And now, they were nothing but lifeless objects, their purpose fulfilled.

But the relics weren't the only thing Elara had lost.

As she stood, her legs unsteady beneath her, she felt a sharp pain in her chest. It was more than just physical exhaustion—it was something deeper, something that tugged at the very core of her being. The magic she had wielded for so long, the power that had carried her through every battle, was gone.

Elara's breath hitched as she realized the full extent of what had happened. In breaking the curse, she had sacrificed her magic. The relics had taken it from her, draining her of the power she had once wielded with such confidence.

Tears pricked at the corners of her eyes as the truth sank in. The magic that had been a part of her for so long was gone, leaving behind only an aching void.

She had saved the kingdom, but she had lost something precious in the process.

Outside the Dark Castle, the kingdom of Eldore was already beginning to feel the effects of the broken curse. The skies, once dark and foreboding, began to clear, the heavy clouds that had lingered over the land for decades dissipating as the light of the sun finally broke through. The trees that had withered under Morgana's dark magic began to bloom once more, their branches heavy with new life. Rivers that had dried up flowed again, and the barren fields that had once stretched across the kingdom were now green with the promise of a new harvest.

The people, too, felt the change. Those who had lived under the shadow of Morgana's reign for so long felt a weight lift from their shoulders, as if the very air they breathed had become lighter. They emerged from their homes, cautiously at first, as if unsure whether the nightmare had truly ended. But as the sun's warmth bathed the land, hope began to blossom in their hearts.

Elara watched from the castle's balcony, her heart heavy with both relief and sorrow. The kingdom was healing. The Dark Queen's curse had been shattered, and the people were free. But the scars of Morgana's reign remained, etched into the land and the hearts of those who had lived through it.

Varian stood beside her, his expression thoughtful as he gazed out over the landscape. "You did it," he said quietly, his voice filled with a mixture of admiration and sadness. "You broke the curse."

Elara nodded, though she didn't feel the triumph that should have accompanied such a victory. "The kingdom is free," she said, her voice soft. "But there's still so much to rebuild."

Varian turned to her, his eyes filled with understanding. "It will take time. The scars left by Morgana's rule run deep. But the people will heal. They always do."

Elara's gaze remained on the horizon, her thoughts swirling with everything that had happened. She had done what she had set out to do—she had freed the kingdom from Morgana's dark magic. But the cost had been higher than she had ever imagined.

"I lost my magic," she said quietly, the words heavy with grief. "It's gone."

Varian's eyes widened slightly in surprise, but he didn't say anything right away. Instead, he placed a comforting hand on her shoulder. "You may have lost your magic, but you saved the kingdom, Elara. That's something no one else could have done."

Elara nodded, though the loss still weighed heavily on her. She had always believed that her magic was a part of who she was, something that defined her. And now, without it, she wasn't sure who she was anymore.

"I just... I thought I would feel different," Elara admitted, her voice barely above a whisper. "I thought that once the curse was broken, everything would be better. But now, I just feel... empty."

Varian's hand tightened on her shoulder, his expression filled with empathy. "It's not easy, letting go of something that's been a part of you for so long. But you're still Elara. You're still the woman who fought her way through every trial, who faced down the Dark Queen and won. You don't need magic to be strong."

Elara's chest tightened at his words, but she forced a small smile. "Thank you, Varian."

He nodded, giving her shoulder one last squeeze before stepping back. "You've done enough for now. Let the kingdom heal. Let yourself heal."

Elara's gaze drifted back to the horizon, her heart still heavy with the weight of all that had happened. She had broken the curse, had freed the kingdom from Morgana's dark reign. But the cost had been great, and the road ahead would not be easy.

The kingdom would heal, but the scars would remain. And Elara would have to find a way to live with the choices she had made.

Days passed, and the kingdom of Eldore slowly began to rebuild. The towns and villages that had suffered under Morgana's rule came to life once more, their people working together to restore what had been lost. The land, freed from the grip of dark magic, began to flourish, and for the first time in decades, hope bloomed in the hearts of the people.

Elara remained at the Dark Castle for a time, overseeing the restoration efforts and offering guidance where she could. But as the days turned into weeks, she began to feel a growing restlessness. The battle was over, but her journey was not. There was still so much she didn't understand about herself, about her place in the world.

One evening, as the sun set over the horizon, painting the sky in shades of gold and crimson, Elara stood alone in the courtyard of the castle. The relics lay in front of her, their once-brilliant light now dim and lifeless. They had served their purpose, but now they, too, were a reminder of what had been lost.

Elara reached out to touch the orb, her fingers brushing against its smooth surface. It was cold now, its magic spent. A pang of sadness gripped her heart, but she knew that it was time to let go.

"I don't need magic to be strong," she whispered to herself, repeating Varian's words.

And as the sun dipped below the horizon, casting the castle in shadow, Elara felt a small spark of hope ignite in her heart.

She had saved the kingdom.

Now, she would begin the journey of saving herself.

Chapter 15: A New Dawn

The first light of dawn stretched across the horizon, bathing the kingdom of Eldore in a soft, golden glow. It had been only weeks since the fall of the Dark Queen, and already, signs of renewal were visible throughout the land. The once-blighted fields were sprouting green shoots, and the rivers that had run dry now flowed with clear water. For the first time in decades, the people of Eldore were breathing freely, their hearts lighter, their fears slowly fading into memory.

But for Elara, standing on the balcony of the castle that had once housed so much darkness, the dawn was bittersweet.

Below her, preparations were being made for a grand celebration. Banners fluttered in the morning breeze, and villagers from every corner of the kingdom had traveled to the capital to honor the one who had freed them from Morgana's reign. The streets were filled with laughter and music, the mood one of festivity and joy. Elara could hear the distant murmur of excited voices as the crowds gathered, eager to see their new hero—the woman who had broken the curse.

Yet, despite the joy that permeated the air, Elara couldn't shake the feeling of melancholy that had settled over her since the final battle. She had done what needed to be done. The kingdom was free, and Morgana's dark magic had been shattered. But the victory had come at a price.

Elara's fingers grazed the railing as she gazed out at the bustling city below. The relics, now nothing more than inert objects, lay in a chest in her room. Their power had been drained, just as hers had. The magic that had once been a part of her, that had flowed through her veins like a lifeblood, was gone. She had sacrificed it to break the curse, and though she had known it was the right choice, the loss still weighed heavily on her.

She no longer felt the hum of magic beneath her skin, the comforting pulse of power that had been with her for as long as she could remember. She was just... Elara now. A woman with no magic, no extraordinary abilities. Just a woman who had made an impossible choice.

A knock on the door pulled her from her thoughts, and she turned to see Varian standing in the doorway, his expression soft but concerned. The pirate captain had been her steadfast ally throughout her journey, and though he was rough around the edges, he had proven to be a true friend.

"They're waiting for you, lass," Varian said, stepping into the room. "The whole kingdom's out there, ready to celebrate their hero."

Elara gave him a small smile, though it didn't quite reach her eyes. "I'm not sure I feel like a hero."

Varian raised an eyebrow, crossing his arms over his chest as he leaned against the doorframe. "You saved the kingdom, Elara. That's more than most people could ever dream of doing."

"I know," Elara said, turning back to the window. "But it doesn't feel like a victory. Not completely."

Varian was silent for a moment before he pushed off the wall and walked over to her, his hand resting on her shoulder. "You lost something in the process," he said quietly. "I get that. But what you did—what you gave up—it wasn't for nothing. Look out there."

Elara followed his gaze, her eyes sweeping over the city. The people were laughing, smiling, their faces lit with the joy of freedom. Children ran through the streets, chasing after one another, their laughter ringing out like music. The weight that had hung over the kingdom for so long was gone, replaced by hope.

"You gave them this," Varian continued, his voice low but steady. "You gave them their lives back."

Elara's chest tightened at his words, but she nodded. She had done what needed to be done, and the kingdom was better for it. But the cost of victory had left her feeling hollow. She had fought so hard, endured so much, and now that it was over, she wasn't sure what came next.

"I guess I just thought it would feel different," Elara admitted, her voice soft. "I thought that once the curse was broken, I would feel... whole. But I don't. I feel lost."

Varian was quiet for a long moment, his gaze thoughtful. "That's because you've spent so long fighting that you've forgotten what it's like to live without the battle. It'll take time to figure out who you are now."

Elara nodded, though she wasn't sure if time alone would be enough to fill the void that had opened within her. The magic she had once relied on was gone, and with it, the sense of purpose that had driven her for so long. She had been the one destined to break the curse, the one foretold by prophecy. But now that the prophecy had been fulfilled, she was left wondering what came next.

"I don't even know where to start," Elara said quietly.

Varian chuckled softly, his hand dropping from her shoulder as he stepped back. "Start by going out there and letting them celebrate you. You've earned it."

Elara gave him a small, grateful smile. He was right, of course. The people needed this celebration, and she owed it to them to be there, even if her heart wasn't entirely in it.

Taking a deep breath, Elara straightened her shoulders and turned to face the door. "Let's get this over with."

The celebration in the capital was unlike anything Elara had ever seen. The streets were lined with banners and flowers, and everywhere she looked, people were smiling, laughing, and dancing. Music filled the air, and vendors handed out food and drinks to the gathered crowds. It was a stark contrast to the grim, oppressive atmosphere that had hung over the kingdom for so long.

As Elara walked through the city, escorted by Varian and a small group of the kingdom's newly appointed guards, people cheered and waved. Children ran up to her, offering flowers and shy smiles, while adults bowed their heads in gratitude. Elara accepted their thanks with a gracious smile, though her heart was heavy with the knowledge of all that had been lost along the way.

She had saved the kingdom, but there were so many who hadn't lived to see this day. Friends and allies who had fallen in battle, victims of Morgana's cruelty who would never know peace. Their faces haunted her, even as the crowds celebrated around her.

At the center of the city, a grand stage had been erected in front of the palace, where the kingdom's leaders awaited her arrival. It was here that Elara would be officially recognized as the hero who had broken the curse, and where the people would celebrate the dawn of a new era.

As she approached the stage, the cheering grew louder, the energy of the crowd swelling like a wave. Elara felt a lump form in her throat as she climbed the steps, her gaze sweeping over the sea of faces below her. These were the people she had fought for, the people she had saved. And yet, she couldn't shake the feeling that she didn't deserve their adoration.

A man dressed in regal robes stepped forward, his face solemn as he addressed the crowd. "People of Eldore," he began, his voice carrying over the din of the crowd. "Today, we gather to celebrate a momentous occasion—the end of a dark and terrible chapter in our history, and the beginning of a new dawn."

The crowd erupted into cheers, and Elara stood silently, her hands clasped in front of her as she listened.

"We owe this victory, this freedom, to one woman—a woman who risked everything to break the curse that bound our kingdom in darkness. She has faced trials and battles that would have broken even the strongest among us, and yet, she stands here today as our hero."

The man turned to Elara, his expression softening as he motioned for her to step forward. "Elara, the people of Eldore owe you a debt that can never be repaid. You have given us our lives back, and for that, we will be forever grateful."

The crowd roared with applause, and Elara felt her cheeks flush as she stepped forward, her heart heavy with the weight of their gratitude. She had never sought recognition or glory—she had only wanted to do what was right. But now, standing before the people she had saved, she realized that their thanks meant more to her than she had expected.

When the applause finally died down, Elara took a deep breath and stepped up to the podium. The crowd fell silent, waiting for her to speak.

"I'm not sure I deserve all of this," Elara began, her voice steady but quiet. "I didn't fight for glory or recognition. I fought because it was the right thing to do. Because this kingdom, our home, deserved to be free."

She paused, her gaze sweeping over the sea of faces. "We've been through so much—together. We've lost people we loved. We've faced darkness that seemed impossible to overcome. And now, we stand on the other side of it, ready to rebuild, ready to move forward."

Elara's throat tightened as she thought of the friends she had lost along the way, the sacrifices that had been made. "But we mustn't forget those who didn't make it here with us. We must honor their memory by living the lives they fought for—lives filled with hope, with kindness, and with the promise of a better future."

The crowd was silent, hanging on her every word.

"I'm not a hero," Elara continued, her voice soft but filled with conviction. "I'm just someone who made a choice. And now, it's up to all of us to make the choice

to rebuild this kingdom, to make it better than it ever was before."

The crowd erupted into cheers once more, and Elara stepped back from the podium, her heart heavy but lighter than it had been before. She still didn't feel like a hero, but she knew that she had done something important. And that was enough.

The celebration lasted long into the night, with the people of Eldore dancing and singing beneath the stars. Elara watched from the palace balcony, a soft smile on her lips as she observed the joy and laughter that filled the streets below. The kingdom was healing. Slowly, but surely, the scars left by Morgana's rule were beginning to fade.

Varian joined her on the balcony, a mug of ale in his hand and a grin on his face. "Quite the party, isn't it?"

Elara chuckled softly, nodding. "It's good to see the people happy again. They've been through so much."

Varian took a sip of his ale, his gaze thoughtful. "And so have you."

Elara didn't respond, but Varian's words echoed in her mind. She had been through so much, had lost so much. But as she stood there, watching the kingdom begin to heal, she realized that she hadn't lost everything.

There was still hope. There was still a future.

And though her journey as the kingdom's savior had come to an end, she knew that her story wasn't over.

The relics, now dormant, still held mysteries that Elara didn't fully understand. And somewhere in the far corners of the kingdom, there were still whispers of forbidden magic, ancient powers that had yet to be uncovered.

Elara didn't know what the future held, but for the first time in a long time, she felt a spark of excitement at the thought of what might come next.

A new dawn had risen over Eldore.

And with it, a new era of magic, mystery, and adventure awaited.

Elara's story was far from finished.

And she was ready for whatever came next.

Don't miss out!

Visit the website below and you can sign up to receive emails whenever Patrick William Lee publishes a new book. There's no charge and no obligation.

https://books2read.com/r/B-A-FLRYB-ICWYE

BOOKS 2 READ

Connecting independent readers to independent writers.

Did you love *The Dark Queen's Curse*? Then you should read *The Blood of the Fallen*[1] by Patrick William Lee!

The Blood of the Fallen is an epic tale of prophecy, sacrifice, and destiny. As a catastrophic battle looms, a hero rises from the ashes of the fallen to unite fractured kingdoms. With the legendary Sword of Legends in hand, the Chosen One must navigate betrayal, forge powerful alliances, and lead an epic struggle against the forces of darkness. This gripping story spans multiple fronts, culminating in a climactic battle that will decide the fate of the world. In the aftermath, the survivors must rebuild and embrace the dawn of a new era, reflecting on the cost of war and the hope for peace.

---

1. https://books2read.com/u/bQ72yZ

2. https://books2read.com/u/bQ72yZ

About the Author

Patrick William Lee is a renowned author celebrated for his enchanting tales of magic and wonder. Specializing in the genres of fairy tales, folk tales, legends, and mythology, Patrick weaves stories that transport readers to fantastical realms where the impossible becomes reality. With a deep love for folklore and a talent for crafting timeless narratives, his books captivate the imaginations of readers young and old. When he's not writing, Patrick enjoys exploring ancient forests, studying mythical creatures, and sharing his passion for storytelling with audiences around the world. His works continue to inspire and delight, leaving a lasting impact on the world of literature.

www.ingramcontent.com/pod-product-compliance
Lightning Source LLC
Chambersburg PA
CBHW022024150726
47990CB00002B/807